D0464713

# BAMBOO KINGDOM

## JOURNEY TO THE DRAGON MOUNTAIN

# BAMBOO KINGDOM

Hunter, Erin, author.
Journey to the Dragon Mountain

2023
33305254130770
ca      01/25/23

# BAMBOO KINGDOM

## JOURNEY TO THE DRAGON MOUNTAIN

# ERIN HUNTER

**HARPER**
*An Imprint of HarperCollinsPublishers*

*Special thanks to Rosie Best*

Bamboo Kingdom #3: Journey to the Dragon Mountain
Copyright © 2023 by Working Partners Ltd.
Series created by Working Partners Ltd.
Map art © 2021 by Virginia Allyn
Interior art © 2021 by Johanna Tarkela
All rights reserved. Printed in the United States of America.
No part of this book may be used or reproduced in any manner whatsoever without written permission except in the case of brief quotations embodied in critical articles and reviews. For information address HarperCollins Children's Books, a division of HarperCollins Publishers, 195 Broadway, New York, NY 10007.
www.harpercollinschildrens.com

ISBN 978-0-06-302204-1

Typography by Corina Lupp

22 23 24 25 26 LBC 5 4 3 2 1

First Edition

*For the doctors, cleaners, farmers, and other essential workers who kept us safe during the pandemic. Thank you.*

*Special thanks to CCPPG for their inspiration and creativity, and for enabling Erin Hunter to bring Bamboo Kingdom to the world.*

DRAGON MOUNTAIN

THE NORTHERN FOREST

FEAST CLEARING

THE SOUTHERN FOREST

# BAMBOO KINGDOM

JOURNEY TO THE DRAGON
MOUNTAIN

# PROLOGUE

SNOWSTORM FELT THE FUR along her back tingle and stand up on end as she padded over the ridge and found herself looking over the snowfield toward the Endless Maw. There were the familiar snowdrifts, the odd tree standing black and stubborn even all the way up here, in the heart of the White Spine Mountains. There were the practice rocks where she had jumped with her littermates, where they'd played at preparing themselves for the transition to adulthood. And there, beyond the rocks, was the edge of the crevasse where their mother had fallen to her death.

That all seemed a long time ago.

It was a perfect day to make the leap. It was cold, but the wind was soft and the sky was like a plain of unbroken pale blue.

She turned back to Frost, waiting for her brother to catch up. It was just the two of them now, and soon she would have to walk away from even him. That was the snow-leopard way. They would each make the jump over the Endless Maw, and on the other side the Snow Cat's paw prints would guide them onto their separate paths. Only the Snow Cat could tell if they would ever see each other again.

*He'll be fine,* she thought. They both would be. They'd already had to survive on their own, since Winter died, hunting their own food and fighting off adult leopards keen to steal their territory. She licked her paw and cleaned her half-mauled ear, feeling a strange pride as her pads brushed the numb scar tissue. That old leopard Flurry had thought it would be easy to take a cave from a pair of vulnerable orphaned cubs, but he'd been wrong.

Frost walked up to stand beside her, and she leaned against him for a moment.

"Ready?" he asked.

"Obviously," she replied.

Frost nodded. "Me too."

But neither of them moved for a few more moments.

"What do you think Shiver and Ghost are doing right now?" Frost asked.

Snowstorm sighed. "I hope they're somewhere warm, and they've got enough to eat. I hope they're together." She scraped one big paw through in the snow, thinking about Shiver's weak lungs and Ghost's tailless, lumbering body. Not for the first time since they left the White Spine, Snowstorm felt a spike of guilt and anxiety for her littermates.

"I miss them," said Frost simply. "I hope they know . . ." He trailed off, but Snowstorm was pretty sure she knew what he was going to say.

*I hope they know we don't blame them for Mother's death.*

Snowstorm hoped that too, but she didn't think it was very likely. She'd told Ghost that it was all his fault, right before he'd left. She'd said some horrible things. He would probably never know she didn't think them anymore. . . .

"Well!" said a voice. "Look who finally got up the courage to come back here!"

Snowstorm spun around and looked up to see a pair of long, fluffy tails dangling from the gnarled branches of a nearby tree. She sighed and rolled her eyes at Frost. It was the cubs Born of Icebound: Brisk and Sleet. They lounged side by side in the tree, tails twitching as they looked down at the cubs Born of Winter.

"Funny, I don't think I've seen you up here since . . ." Sleet pretended to stop and think. "Oh, that's right—since the last time one of you freaks tried the leap."

"Didn't go too well, did it?" said Brisk.

"Are you off to join Winter at the bottom of the Maw?" Sleet sneered.

Snowstorm sprang into a run. She pounded across the snow, right at the tree where the two leopards were sitting. At once, the cubs Born of Icebound scrambled to their paws, ears pinned back with fear. Brisk climbed onto a higher branch, and Sleet braced himself, tucking his tail up out of reach just as Snowstorm got to the tree trunk and made a swipe for it.

"Strong words from a pair of cubs who haven't even tried the leap," Frost said evenly, following behind her at a stroll.

"They don't *need* to leap the Maw," Snowstorm snarled, pacing around the tree trunk. "Our mother may be dead, but at least we've learned to look after ourselves. These two will be living in Icebound's cave until their fur falls out!"

Sleet growled. Snowstorm crouched as if she were going to pounce up into the tree, and Sleet's growls turned into a yelp as he clawed his way onto the higher branch, jostling for space with Brisk.

Snowstorm relaxed.

"Come on," she said to Frost. "We're adult leopards now. We don't need to fight with cubs anymore."

She turned away, and she and Frost set out together over the snow, ignoring the hisses of Brisk and Sleet. She'd mostly said it to annoy them, but it was true, too. On the other side of the Endless Maw they would be real adults, and nothing the cubs Born of Icebound could say would change that.

Her heart started to beat harder as they approached the edge of the crevasse. Flickers of memory came back to her, the horrible and wonderful all mixed together: Winter's body falling from the slippery ledge, Winter fighting Icebound to keep them safe, Ghost climbing safely out of the Maw, the terrible things she had said to him. She took a deep breath and raised her head. The memories couldn't weigh her down now.

Even though the day was bright and the weather still, the Endless Maw was so deep that the bottom was wreathed in shadow. There was no sign of Winter's bones—of course, they would have been long buried in the snow by now—but Snowstorm allowed herself one glance anyway. Then she focused on the column of rock that stood in the middle of the chasm. It looked much closer than it had when she was a little cub. Confidence started to grow in her chest. She could do this.

"Go on," Frost said, his ears flicking with amusement. "You go first—you always do."

She briefly licked her brother on the forehead. "I'll see you on the other side."

Then she backed up from the edge, crouched, ran, and leaped. Her heart gave a thump in midair, so hard she could feel it in the pads of her paws, and then she landed in the snow on the top of the column. She didn't pause or look back, but bunched her muscles and leaped again, sailing through the air. Her front paws slammed down on the far edge of the Maw and she pushed herself forward, running a few steps into the flattened snow before circling back to watch her brother.

Frost looked very small from this side of the Maw. The practice rocks and the gnarled trees seemed tiny.

Frost crouched, wiggling his tail behind him. Snowstorm dug her claws into the snow.

*Come on, Frost. You can do it.*

He leaped. It was a good, strong jump, and he made it to

the column with paw-lengths to spare. He skidded a tiny bit on the top of the rock, but didn't stop moving, and with a last strong push he jumped from the column.

He wasn't going to make it. Snowstorm knew it at once. She rushed to the edge as she saw the expression in Frost's eyes change, the arc of his leap carrying him down. She saw his claws come out, a desperate attempt to reach the edge of the chasm. And he did, by a single claw-length, the rest of his body falling too far and slamming into the wall of the Maw. He scratched and scrabbled at the rocks, one of his claws splintering with the impact. Snowstorm threw herself forward in the same moment and snapped at him.

Her teeth closed in the scruff of Frost's neck, and she bunched her muscles and scrambled backward in the snow to stop them both from falling over the edge and crashing to the rocks below. With a roar of effort, she backed away. Frost got a paw onto the snow, and then another, and then they were flying backward, tumbling over and over in a wild ball of fur and claws.

They came to a stop against a snowdrift, and lay there panting in a tangled heap, too stunned by the terror of what had almost happened to speak at first.

Then there was a yelp from across the Maw. "They did it!"

Snowstorm looked over and saw Brisk and Sleet, looking tiny on the other side of the crevasse. Brisk's tail was lashing with excitement, but it stopped when Sleet batted her ear with his paw.

"Just barely," he sneered, loud enough that Snowstorm could hear him clearly over the Maw. "Good thing she was there to save his tail one last time, huh?"

Brisk sniggered.

"Speaking of my tail, I think you're sitting on it," said Frost.

Snowstorm wriggled to her paws and tried not to look as shaken as she felt.

"We made it," she said. "We're adults now."

"Right," said Frost. "I guess that means . . ."

The snow shifted under Snowstorm's feet. For a moment she thought it was just her own paws, still unsteady with shock. But then it shifted again, and a low rumble filled the air, growing until it sounded like the roar of a creature as big as the mountain. Frost nudged his head against her shoulder, and they both stumbled away from the edge of the Maw as a sheet of snow crumpled and fell in. Across the gap, Brisk and Sleet scrambled backward too and fled across the snowfield.

"It's just an earthquake," Frost said, pressing himself against Snowstorm. "Right?"

"It must be," she said. But she wasn't so sure. The ground shook, but the noise filled the air until it sounded like the Snow Cat itself, roaring in anger. She looked around. It was bad to be caught in an earthquake in unfamiliar territory. There could be an avalanche, or a rockfall. The open snowfield didn't feel safe, but she didn't want to get any closer to the small, jagged peaks nearby. . . .

Then she spotted something on the horizon. Another

peak, huge and far off, its slopes seeming purple . . . and smoke rising from the summit.

"What *is* that?" she gasped.

Frost followed her gaze and shook his head. "Is the Snow Cat angry about something?"

"Or is it warning us that danger is coming?" Snowstorm wondered. "I don't like the look of that smoke."

She looked around at the unfamiliar landscape once again, and then down at her brother's tail, which had curled itself between her front legs and over her paws.

"Frost?" she said. "I think . . . this isn't a good time to split up. I don't think the Snow Cat wants us wandering off alone. Do you want to stick together for now? Just for a bit?"

Frost was already nodding before she'd finished speaking.

"Whatever's going on," he said, "I think we ought to face it together. That's what the Snow Cat would want."

"It's what Mother would want too," Snowstorm added quietly.

They stood together, braced against the rumbling earth, their eyes fixed on the smoking purple mountain in the distance.

*Please, Snow Cat,* Snowstorm thought. *Let Ghost and Shiver be safe too. . . .*

# CHAPTER ONE

RAIN SAT IN THE mud and stared up at the white panda, a growl of annoyance rumbling in her throat. Ghost stared back with the same vexed expression he always wore. All she could see at the top of the pit was his wide, white face, the branches of trees, and a gray streak of sky.

"What do you want now?" Rain snarled.

Beside her, Peony stirred from her doze and raised her head. She saw Ghost and let out a derisive snort and rolled over to stare at the wall of the pit. It had been their prison for several days now—Rain's punishment for revealing to the other pandas that Sunset was not the Dragon Speaker he claimed to be. *Not that anyone believed me anyway,* Rain thought sourly. They had turned on her and Peony, her mother, and had done nothing to stop Sunset's monkey servants from forcing them into the pit.

"Sunset's on his way," said Ghost.

He always spoke to her like that, direct and short. Rain had expected him to be more like Sunset, smirking and gloating over having Rain as his prisoner, but he'd mostly ignored her.

*He's just a thug, here to smack us back down if we try to climb out of this pit. Sunset's the brains.*

"Oh yeah? And what do you want me to do about it?" Rain snapped. "Maybe I should try to clean up a bit? Oh, wait." She splashed her paws in the muddy puddles at the bottom of the pit. "I can't—it's a hole in the ground."

"Sunset could make it much worse for you down there," Ghost pointed out.

"Yeah," said a voice, and a squashed blue face peered over the edge. One of Brawnshanks's crew of golden monkeys. Rain thought this was the one called Jitterpaws. She was eating a yellow gingko fruit—the fourth one Rain had seen her chewing on so far today. "You'd better behave, or it won't just be fruit and stuff we throw down there. We've been collecting rocks specially."

Rain felt a jolt of misgiving at this, but she tried not to let it show. "With your aim? You couldn't hit a golden takin if you were standing right next to it," she sneered.

"You wait and see," said Jitterpaws. "Maybe we'll throw Ghost down there, let the two of you fight it out, huh?" She prodded Ghost in the ribs. He growled at her, and she chittered and skipped away from him.

"Two of us against one of you? I don't like your chances,

even if you are Sunset's white monster," Rain said.

Ghost tilted his head. "You're both starving. You must be stiff from lying in a puddle for days."

"And I suppose you're all toughened up from doing Sunset's dirty work for him," Rain said.

Ghost frowned, and Rain thought she'd hit a nerve.

"Do you even know where I come from? I learned to fight with Winter, the best snow-leopard hunter in the White Spine Mountains. If I wanted to . . ." He shook his head. "Do you always start fights you can't win?"

*Yes, always,* Rain thought. "Ooh, trained by leopards," she said out loud. "I'm sure if Sunset has you chasing goats and rabbits, that'll come in very useful."

"You really don't ever shut up, do you?" Ghost said.

"Why don't you come down here and stop me?" Rain retorted.

"Cubs, cubs," said a low, amused voice. Rain sat back down, and Peony rolled over and sat up as Sunset's large black-and-white face peered over the edge of the pit. Ghost took a respectful step back. "There's no need for any of that, as long as you cooperate."

"Never," Rain barked. "What could you want from us anyway? We can't exactly do much from down here."

"You say you're a Dragon Speaker," Sunset said. "I want you to tell me your prophecies."

"And why should I?"

"Because there are many more ways I can make your life

miserable down there," growled Sunset. "I'm giving you one chance. Tell me a prophecy, or there will be consequences."

*What prophecy?* Rain thought. *I haven't had a single vision since I've been down here. And I've been trying. . . .*

But she refused to let Sunset know that. She thought for a moment, staring at Sunset, and the tips of Ghost's ears, and Jitterpaws's tail, which she could see over the edge of the pit. . . .

"All right, here's a prophecy for you." Rain held out her paws and shut her eyes. She hesitated as she remembered a simpler time, when she'd pretended to give out prophecies to the Prosperhill cubs—usually to get out of doing chores. "The Dragon speaks to me, and it says . . . one of your monkeys is going to be sick."

She opened her eyes and beamed at Sunset just in time to catch his face falling from hopeful interest to rage.

*"Fine,"* he growled, his low voice rumbling. "If you won't—"

"Actually . . . ," piped up Jitterpaws. She pressed one paw to her stomach, the other still clutching her fifth gingko fruit of the day. "I do feel a bit . . ." She turned away, and there was a squeaky retching sound.

*Right on cue.* Rain smirked up at Sunset.

"Very funny," he snarled, one eye twitching. "I hope you enjoy being on reduced meals. The monkeys will feed you *half* of what they've been giving you so far, until you come up with something real." He turned away, not waiting for Rain's reply, and Ghost went with him.

Rain glanced at Peony, suddenly uncertain. Her adoptive mother's shoulders had slumped at the mention of food. But she had no real prophecy to tell him. . . .

Peony noticed Rain looking at her and sighed. "It's all right, Rain. You did the right thing. We just need to find a way out of here."

"Here you go, stupid pandas," called out a monkey voice from above—it wasn't Jitterpaws, but a different young female. "Half your rations, coming up!"

Six gingko fruits thudded into the soft mud beside Rain.

She looked up, frowning in confusion. They'd had six last time too, so shouldn't it have been three? Not that she was planning to tell the monkey that. . . .

But the golden monkey looking down into the pit had a familiar face. Rain couldn't place it for a second, and then her memory kicked in.

*Nimbletail.* She was the young female Rain had noticed gathering the striped bamboo for Sunset, the same one who'd then caught Rain trying to cross the river and hadn't said anything to the others she was with.

*Why are you helping me?* Rain wondered. But as she opened her mouth to speak, Nimbletail put a long brown finger to her lips. She leaned right over the edge of the pit.

"You have to try to come up with a prophecy," she whispered. "Something convincing. Or Brawnshanks will be angry with you as well as Sunset—and you don't want that." She straightened and picked up the stone from inside Jitterpaws's gingko. "Enjoy, prisoners!" she said, much louder, and threw the stone into the pit—missing Rain by a whole bear-length. Before Rain could say anything, she'd vanished.

Rain and Peony exchanged surprised glances. Rain quickly passed a gingko to her mother and hid the rest behind her back, in case one of the other monkeys happened to look over into the pit.

"What time is it now?" Peony asked her. Rain squinted up at the sky. The sun had passed over them long ago, and the light was beginning to dim.

"I think it's probably Dying Light," she guessed.

Peony nodded sadly. Rain knew it pained her not to be able to observe the feasts at their proper time. Rain was pretty certain the Dragon wouldn't mind, considering the circumstances, but for some reason her reassurances hadn't cheered Peony up much.

"At the Feast of Dying Light, your humble pandas bow before you. Thank you for the gift of the gingko fruit and the kindness you bestow upon us."

Rain bowed her head and waited politely for Peony to finish, before chewing down on the stinky yellow flesh and hard gingko nut. They ate in silence; then, after Rain checked that it was safe, she passed Peony a second fruit. Her mother sighed before she took another bite. Rain knew exactly how she felt. She longed for a taste of bamboo. It hurt to know that there were forests of it just out of reach at the top of their pit.

"I can't just get an actual prophecy like that, or I would

have by now," Rain said under her breath. "I guess I can make something up, something that sounds real. I just don't know if I can fool Sunset. But I have to get us out of this, somehow. . . ."

"We'll get out of it together," her mother reminded her.

"Yes—but I'm the one who's a Dragon Speaker," she replied. It still felt strange to say it out loud.

*I wish Leaf could hear me say that,* she thought. *Even though she'd probably be really annoying and nice and not even gloat about the fact that she was right. If I'd listened to her on the mountain, would we still be in this pit?*

They saved the final fruits for the Feast of Moon Climb, and sure enough, the monkeys didn't give them anything else to eat before the light faded completely and the tree branches above were swallowed up in darkness. Rain could just make out Peony's white fur against the black walls of the pit as they quietly gave thanks to the Dragon and split one of the fruits in half so that they'd still have one left for the Feast of Moon Fall.

Afterward, Peony lay down again with her head tucked under her paws, and though she didn't fall asleep right away, eventually her breathing turned slow and deep. Rain sat up, wide awake, listening to her stomach rumbling. She heard the sound of the guard monkeys swapping for new ones— she could always tell when this happened, because at least one monkey would pick a fight with one of the others, and then things would calm down again. She listened for their chattering to slow and stop.

All was silent for a while. The birds and small creatures of the forest were silent too. Even the wind was still.

Rain got up, stretching out as much as she could. Ghost was right—she was stiff. But she still had to do this.

She hadn't made it last night, or the night before that. Another reason to wish that Leaf were here—her sister would probably have scaled the slippery mud-and-rock walls with no problem. But Leaf wasn't here, so Rain had to try.

It wasn't completely hopeless. She'd learned that on her previous attempts. She'd found that one of the sides of the pit had better paw holds than the others, with a few large rocks and tree roots sticking out from the earth. She knew that if she could just get her claws around the curved root that was *almost* out of her reach, she could pull herself up so all her paws were off the ground.

She clung on to the root and dragged herself up. Her back paws scrambled and kicked at the mud, and she desperately tried to keep breathing evenly so her frightened panting wouldn't wake the monkeys. Finally she found a rock to stand on and pushed herself up, earth coating the fur on her stomach. She looked up. She could only just make out the edge of the pit in the darkness. She could do this. There was another stone for her to step onto, and then, over to her right, if she leaned dangerously on another root that wobbled as she gripped it, she could dig her claws into the exposed tunnel of a pika warren that Sunset had ruthlessly dug through when he'd made the pit.

She was so close. Only a bear-length to go now, and she was higher up than she'd made it on previous nights. If she could just—

She looked up again, and saw something glinting in the darkness. A pair of slitted eyes, looking right at her from the top of the pit.

She jolted in surprise and her back paw slid out from under her. She lost her grip and fell. It wasn't a terribly long distance, but it still knocked the wind out of her as she thumped down into the mud with a splash. She panted, trying to get her breath back, and stared up at the place where the eyes had been. They were gone now.

*Shadowhunter?*

*No . . . they were like his, but different. I think that creature was smaller. And he'd have said something to me; he wouldn't have just vanished. Right?*

She waited, her heart beating in her throat, but the creature had melted into the darkness without even so much as a snort or the padding of paws.

Rain shuddered.

It wasn't just Ghost up there, or Sunset, or the golden monkeys. Something else was out there in the dark too. And it was watching them.

# CHAPTER TWO

LEAF GIGGLED AND SCAMPERED down the slope. Her paws were aching a little from walking, but they felt light and happy underneath her. It was a sunny morning, and her newfound brother, Pepper, was walking beside her. She had found him— the final triplet! All they needed to do now was find Rain, and then there would be nothing standing between them and fulfilling their destinies as Dragon Speakers. The idea was thrilling and frightening all at once.

"There's water here!" Dasher called, and Leaf nudged Pepper as she headed toward her red panda friend's voice. They found him standing with his front paws in a clear mountain stream, and joined him to lap at the lovely cool waters.

When they'd quenched their thirst, Leaf shook the drops from her muzzle and sat down to scratch behind her ear.

"Where do you think Rain and Plum are now?" she asked Dasher.

"Rain was always saying she wanted to confront Sunset," Dasher said. "Maybe she persuaded Plum to go there first. Maybe she tried to cross the river? The water level's gone down so much, perhaps she made it!"

Leaf's heart sank a little at this thought. She'd tried to convince her sister not to face the false Dragon Speaker alone, but Rain wasn't one to be talked out of something once she'd made up her mind. "I hope she hasn't gotten herself in trouble. We should go to the Southern Forest and look for her there. Maybe we can stop her making a terrible mistake."

"No!" Pepper squeaked. Leaf turned to look at him. "I mean, no, I don't think she's in the Southern Forest. I think I saw her. Here. On this side of the river."

"What?" Leaf gasped. "You did? Where?"

"And why didn't you say anything?" Dasher frowned. "I thought Leaf was the first one of the triplets you've met."

"Oh, she is—I didn't *meet* Rain," Pepper said. "So much has happened, I've been confused. . . . But I think I saw her. It was before I'd run into the monkeys and found out what our white grip pads meant, so I saw it and I didn't think anything of it. . . ." He sighed and licked sadly at the scab that had formed over the skin where his own grip pad should have been. Leaf winced. The poor thing had been so afraid of being caught by the monkeys that he'd bitten his own pad off. She couldn't imagine how scared he must have been to do that.

Dasher looked like he wanted to ask more questions, but Leaf didn't want to upset Pepper any more, so she threw Dasher a quieting glance.

"It's all right," she said to Pepper. "We'll protect you from them. As soon as we find Rain, nobody will be able to hurt us. Where did you see her? Was she with an older panda?"

"I didn't see another panda. Rain was by a dried-up river-bed," Pepper said. "In, um . . ." He looked around. "In the east of the Northern Forest."

"Then let's go!" Leaf said, and gave Pepper a gentle nudge with her nose. "We'll find Rain, and then everything will be all right. You'll see."

As they wound between and over the sparse hills of the Northern Forest, Leaf kept her eyes peeled for a sign: either a sign that Rain had been here—a scent or a paw print—or some message from the Dragon. She had seen its scaly body leave a trail in the pine needles when they'd been lost in the mountains, and she was sure that its bats had led her first to the Darkpool and the other Slenderwood pandas, and then to Pepper. Perhaps there would be another sign waiting for her at this dried-up riverbed. Perhaps Pepper himself would be the one to see it! This thought put a spring in her paws.

"Tell us all about yourself, Pepper!" she said. "Where did you grow up? Did you have an aunt or someone looking after you, like I had Aunt Plum?"

"I was alone for a long time," Pepper said. "I remember

being a very tiny cub, so small I didn't even have fur. I remember seeing two other cubs lying next to me—that must have been you and Rain!"

"Wow," Leaf breathed. "I don't remember that far back! Do you remember our mother, Orchid?"

"Oh yes," Pepper said.

"I wish I did," Leaf sighed. "I'm so glad one of us does. Please, tell me, what do you remember about her?"

"She smelled like fresh bamboo," said Pepper dreamily. "Her fur was as soft as the dew, and her eyes . . . they were very light, golden brown. Like amber."

"Wow," said Leaf again. She could picture Orchid in her mind, a quiet smile on her muzzle, licking the three tiny pink cubs as they nestled against her soft fur. But Pepper could actually *remember* it.

"You don't remember being a little cub in that much detail, Leaf?" Dasher asked.

"No, I don't remember Mother at all," said Leaf sadly.

"Me neither," said Dasher. His voice sounded slightly strange, and when Leaf looked over to him, she saw that his long stripy tail was curling and lashing behind him in agitation. "In fact, I've never heard of anyone remembering so far back, not that clearly."

"I guess it is odd," Pepper chuckled. "Maybe it's something to do with being a Dragon Speaker?"

"We do all have our strengths," Leaf said. "I'm a climber; Rain's a swimmer. Maybe Pepper's memory is his strength!"

"Yeah, maybe," Dasher said, and his tail relaxed.

Leaf hung back and let Pepper get a little way ahead, so she could whisper to Dasher.

"I know he's a bit odd," she said. "But think of it this way—isn't it better than having to stop to argue with Rain every few steps?"

Dasher sniggered. "I suppose that's true!"

"She's my sister and I love her," Leaf added quickly, "but it's a relief to be traveling with someone who *gets* it!"

They kept moving east, pausing for feasts and occasionally stopping to let Pepper get his bearings and point them in the right direction. Leaf pointed out the way to the Darkpool, where she had last seen the Slenderwood pandas and the red pandas, and Pepper told her that he thought they should veer north.

The area he led them into was more thickly forested than the Slenderwood, but it didn't feel at all lush or welcoming. It was as if winter had come to this part of the forest early: The ground was carpeted with crunchy fallen leaves and pine needles, broken up by the occasional jagged rock. But even though many of the tree branches were bare, they twisted together so thickly that they cast dark, strange shadows over the whole hillside. They had only just stopped for the Feast of Long Light, but it felt more like Moon Climb under the canopy of this forest.

"This place feels weird," Dasher said, sniffing suspiciously at a rock. "Do you feel a bit like . . ."

"Like what?" Leaf asked. The truth was, she *was* feeling a bit strange. The shadows seemed to shift around her, and not in the friendly way that suggested a sinuous, scaly body might be close by, but more like how a shadow would move if it was trying not to be seen. Was she just imagining it?

"I don't know . . . I just don't like it," Dasher said. "Why would Rain come here?"

"Pepper?" Leaf prompted. "Are you sure we're going the right way?"

"Definitely," said Pepper, putting his head down in determination. "I know it's a bit scary, but we just have to keep going."

They hardly saw any bamboo as they crept farther into this dead-seeming forest, but whenever Leaf spotted a green shoot pressing up through the brown earth, she made sure to collect it and carry it with her in her jaws, so when it was time to stop for the Feast of Sun Fall, they at least had a few scraps of bamboo to eat.

Dasher hurried off to hunt for something to eat for himself. Leaf was glad she didn't have to eat the beetles or moss he would probably find—and Dasher knew better than to offer her a share in any mice or fish he caught, even though he was perfectly happy to eat them if there was no fruit or fungus growing nearby. Still, her stomach rumbled as she pawed at the small pile of bamboo she'd managed to collect.

"Come on, let's see if there's any more nearby," she told Pepper. "Just while Dasher's gone."

But they had hardly sniffed around the closest trees before Dasher came skidding back through the trunks and rolled to a jittery halt beside Leaf.

"What's the matter?" she asked, her fur prickling, staring at the part of the forest he'd come from.

"I heard something," Dasher muttered.

"What kind of something?"

Dasher shook his head and trod down the crunchy ground with his front paws. "I'm not sure. Something moving. It sounded . . . heavy."

"Heavy like a panda?" Leaf prompted. "Could it have been Rain?"

"More like several pandas. Or several something elses. I don't know, Leaf. I didn't like it."

"Maybe we should go and see what it was," Pepper chirped, and took a few confident paw steps into the forest. Leaf's heart gave a heavy jolt.

"No, Pepper! Wait. Let's just wait and listen for a moment?"

Pepper shrugged and sat down. Leaf let out a shaky sigh of relief. He was very brave, but she couldn't let her only brother go running into the woods alone!

She tried to focus on listening to the sounds of the forest. There were rustles among the leaves, and the shadows shifted a little, but there were no big, heavy creatures rushing toward them.

"I think it might be all right," Leaf said, and tried to give Dasher an encouraging lick on the top of his head. Dasher nodded, but he was still kneading the leaves with one paw. He looked up at Leaf.

"Can I have some of your bamboo? Instead of going back out there and looking for something else?" he asked.

Pepper frowned, but Leaf nodded.

"Of course," she said. They sat down together, and she recited the blessing before passing out a third of the bamboo to each of them. Pepper ate his in a few quick chomps, but Leaf tried to make hers last a bit longer. She wasn't sure if there would be anything at all to eat at Moon Climb or Moon Fall.

"I'm thirsty," said Pepper. He turned to Dasher. "Did you see any water over there?"

"Not much," Dasher said. "There was a muddy place, with some puddles."

"That'll have to do," said Leaf. "But we'll all go together. Just in case."

"All right." Dasher's tail dragged apprehensively behind him as they got to their paws and started to walk through the trees.

The watery place wasn't far, and it was very clear to Leaf when they were getting close—her paws started to make soft sucking sounds as she lifted them up, and soon the crunchy leaves gave way to a wide hollow filled with dark brown mud. Dasher was right: There were a few puddles of clear water around the edges. Pepper trotted over, slipping a little on the mud, and immediately began to drink. Leaf walked more carefully after him, and lapped at the surface of the next puddle.

Suddenly there was a loud snort, and Leaf's paws skidded in the mud as she jumped and looked up. Across the hollow, two shapes were emerging from the trees. They had thick, bristled hides and long tusks that curved in front of their snouts.

"Boars!" Dasher yelped.

Each of them was as big as Leaf, if not bigger, and both of them looked furious.

"Hey!" one of the boars rumbled. "You, bears!" He stepped forward and stomped his hard trotter on the ground, sending up a shower of mud.

The other roared. "This is our wallow! Get out!" He lowered his head, tusks pointed right at Leaf, and surged forward.

"Get back—the trees, get in the trees!" Leaf yelped. Dasher was already scrambling up the nearest trunk, but Pepper was simply staring at the charging boar, as if he didn't understand the oncoming danger. Leaf head-butted him hard in the side, and he stumbled and then seemed to come back to his senses, running for the trunk of the next tree along.

Leaf dug her claws into the bark and pushed herself up with all her strength. The twisted trunks of the trees felt like they'd been sent from the Dragon as her back paws quickly found paw holds and she scrambled onto the first thick branch, and then the next. The tree shook, and she clung with all her might to the branch and looked down. The boar had slammed his head into the trunk, and was panting and snorting up at her with red rage in his eyes.

But the boars couldn't climb trees—their trotters wouldn't be able to keep their grip. Leaf was safe.

She looked around, desperately hoping to see Pepper and Dasher in the branches nearby. Dasher's striped tail hung down from the very top of his tree, shuddering as he made an attempt to growl back at the boar. But where was Pepper?

"Go away!" squeaked a frightened voice from somewhere on Leaf's left side. She wiggled around on her branch to look at the next tree, and saw Pepper leaning over from a low branch, shouting down at the second boar, who was circling it and growling. Leaf's heart thumped as she watched him—he looked like any moment he might lose his balance, tip over, and fall right onto the boar's tusks! But then he righted himself and climbed up onto a higher branch.

"This is our wallow! You get your own!" The first boar snorted up at Leaf again.

"We don't want your wallow!" Leaf snapped back. "We're leaving. Don't try to follow us!"

Pepper looked over at Leaf, his ears pressed back in startled fear. "I'm not going back down there until these big pigs go away. . . ."

"Well, we're not going away until you come down!" retorted the boar.

Leaf climbed up and peered through the thick, dry canopy. Then she leaned down to call to Pepper.

"We can go through the tree branches. If that's all right with you?" she added, a little sarcastically, to the two boars. "We'll be on our way up here—you won't see us at your wallow again."

The boars looked at each other and sniffed. "Fine," said one.

Leaf began to lead the way, working her way along the branches and stepping carefully into the next tree without too much difficulty. Dasher and Pepper followed her, casting nervous looks back at the boars as they went.

"Ignore them," Leaf whispered, waiting for Pepper to catch up so she could help him with a tricky reach. "Just look where you're going, and pretend they're already far behind us."

Pepper nodded, for once seeming to have nothing to say, and inched along his bowing branch until he could hop clumsily onto the next. They kept moving, with Leaf scouting out branches that would take her weight and then pausing to let Pepper and Dasher catch up, until they lost sight of the boars and the hollow altogether, and were climbing over crunchy fallen leaves once more.

"Which direction is the dried-up river from here?" she asked Pepper, after he'd managed a tricky crossing into a new tree. Pepper peered down at the forest, looking around as if searching for a landmark to navigate by. Leaf held her breath, hoping they hadn't lost Rain's trail thanks to those grumpy boars.

But while they were both staring down at the ground,

Dasher edged along the branch next to Leaf and put his front paws on her leg.

"Leaf," he said very quietly, "I think I can hear something."

"Is it the boars?" Leaf asked. "Are they following us?" She looked back, straining to listen. She usually had quite good hearing, but apart from the creak of branches moving in the breeze, there was nothing.

"I think it's something else," Dasher said, and then lowered his voice even further. "Up here, in the trees, with us!"

"It's that way!" Pepper exclaimed, gesturing with his nose. Leaf and Dasher both cringed at how loud his voice was.

"Come on, let's go," Leaf said. "And whatever it is, let's hope it's like the boars and we can get out of its territory quick."

She led them into the next tree, but with Dasher's warning echoing in her mind, she started to weave left and right, zigzagging in the general direction Pepper had pointed, but maybe, hopefully, erratically enough that their trail would be confused.

But Dasher didn't seem any less on edge. And after a few more clambers between the branches, Leaf suddenly saw Pepper sit up tall and look behind him. She held her breath and, sure enough, there was a faint rustling from behind them.

They hurried onward, keeping an eye out for the easiest point to get down out of the trees—they had lost the boars now, and they would be faster on foot. Finally she found a tree whose trunk leaned over at such a steep angle that she could walk down it to the ground, and she let Pepper and Dasher run down in front of her, standing with her claws in the bark and her eyes fixed on the treetops behind them. Was that a flash of movement, a few trees back? The sound of scrabbling feet, and branches bending under the weight of . . . something?

"The river's close now!" Pepper said, and set off running through the crunchy leaves, with Leaf and Dasher right behind him.

They were moving faster, but Leaf was sure that whatever had been following them through the trees wouldn't lose them that easily. To her relief, they only had to crest one more ridge before they were looking down at what was unmistakably a dried-up riverbed: a channel of drying mud that ran down the hill and out of sight.

"This is it! This is where I saw Rain," said Pepper proudly. He sat down on the edge of the channel and licked his paws, as if their mission were finished and they had nothing more to do. Leaf frowned, and glanced up into the trees. Was that branch moving under something's paws, or was it just the wind?

"Pepper!" she hissed. "Help me search for Rain's scent!"

"Oh, right," said Pepper, and began to delicately sniff the ground around him. Leaf ran into the middle of the dry river and searched as fast as she could, waiting for the slightest hint that her sister had been here.

"What was she doing when you saw her?" she asked Pepper, as she ran from one side of the muddy channel to the other. "Was she moving quickly? Maybe she climbed one of the trees?"

Dasher was going from tree to tree, sniffing around each one in turn. He turned away from the one he'd been investigating and gave Pepper a stare.

"Are you *sure* you saw her here?" he snapped.

"Of course he did," Leaf said, but she threw Pepper a fearful look. Pepper nodded at her, and she sagged a little with relief. "He's just trying to help, Dasher. Maybe she was only here briefly and we just need to keep going."

"You're not going nowhere," said a voice from right behind her. Leaf spun around, but there was no one there—until there was a blur of gold and a thump, and she found herself nose to flattened nose with a golden monkey, its blue face contorted in a smirk. She turned again to warn the others, but it was too late. Monkeys dropped from the trees all around them, thudding into the leaves, some of them snorting with laughter. Pepper twitched and hunkered down, and Dasher spun in a circle, his tail lashing.

Leaf backed away from the golden monkey, her lips parting in a snarl, bracing herself to toss aside the first monkey who tried to jump on her. But none of them moved.

"What do you want?" she growled. "Are you Sunset's minions?"

The monkey looked her up and down, and then casually stepped toward her and sniffed. "This isn't the one we're looking for," she said.

"Quickfingers, I've got him!" chittered one of the others, and Leaf turned to see the monkeys surrounding Pepper. "This is the one! He's here!"

Pepper looked terrified. "No," he said. "I don't know what you're talking about. I'm nobody. I've never been to the Southern Forest!"

"You leave him alone!" Leaf roared, and started to charge at the monkeys. To her surprise, she met no resistance as she skidded to Pepper's side—the monkeys leaped out of the way, and some of them climbed back into the trees.

"We got what we came for," said Quickfingers.

"Can't wait to tell Brawnshanks about this," sniggered one of the others. He gave Pepper a mocking bow of the head, and then the monkeys were leaping up into the branches. In a matter of moments they had vanished, leaving nothing but shifting shadows behind them.

"What was that?" Dasher yelped, looking from Leaf to Pepper and back, his tail still twitching in agitation.

"And who's Brawnshanks?" Leaf muttered. "Is that another monkey?"

"I . . . I don't know," said Pepper. He shuddered, then shook himself hard from ears to tail.

"Why did they just leave?" Leaf wondered out loud. "Didn't you say they attacked you before? And how did they know who you were? They didn't even look at your grip pad or anything!"

"I don't know!" Pepper said in a strangled voice.

"If you want to know what I think," said Dasher, slowly

approaching Pepper, "I think Pepper's not telling us everything. We can't trust him, Leaf. He led us here, and there's no sign of Rain, but suddenly there are monkeys? He's only taken us into danger!"

Pepper didn't say anything, but he looked absolutely stricken, turning eyes full of fear on Leaf.

"Dasher, no," Leaf said, hurrying to her brother's side. "Look at him—he's terrified. He's trying to help. It's not his fault the monkeys followed us here. You need to stop being so suspicious."

Dasher huffed derisively and started to clean between his toes. "I don't trust him."

"Dasher!" Leaf snapped. "Please, don't be like this. No harm was done, was it? The monkeys left us alone."

"I promise I don't know why those monkeys did what they did," Pepper said in a small voice. "We—we should keep looking for our sister. She probably passed through here a while ago. I can show you where she was heading. . . ."

Dasher sighed and rolled his eyes. "All right. Let's go, then. And hope those monkeys can't pick up our trail when they come back."

"I think Rain went this way," Pepper said, surprisingly brightly, and trotted across the dry river and toward a gap between the trees.

Leaf hung back a little with Dasher, who looked at Pepper's sprightly steps and then up at her with a quizzical frown on his small face.

"Whatever else you think of him, you've got to admit, he's a bit weird," he said.

Leaf sighed. "Maybe. But he's my brother, Dash. And he's our only hope of finding Rain."

# CHAPTER THREE

GHOST TRUDGED UP THE panda path toward the feast clearing. There was a group of pandas gathered at one of the turns, chatting, relaxed, as if everything were normal in the Southern Forest. But as Ghost approached, one by one they noticed him and fell silent. Even the cubs, Fir and Frog, stopped playing as he drew closer. Horizon put her paw on Fir's shoulder and pulled her cub firmly toward her, and away from him.

He'd never felt so alone. Sunset had befriended him, made him feel that finally he belonged—and then betrayed him. By the time Ghost had come to realize that Sunset was a liar and a murderer who had tricked the Bamboo Kingdom into believing he was the Dragon Speaker, it had been too late. Sunset had turned Ghost into his devoted servant, and made the other pandas frightened of him. There was no one he could confide in—no one who would believe him. He'd never missed Shiver, his littermate, more, but he had driven her away.

*All because of Sunset,* he thought bitterly. *All for his lies.*

Now he didn't try to challenge or greet the other pandas. He wasn't surprised when they leaned away from him as he passed, or even when Lily flinched as he glanced up and met her eyes.

*Murderer,* he thought. *White monster. Killer of pandas. That's what they all think of me now. I would be afraid of a panda like that too.*

Sunset had ordered Ghost to kill Pepper, the strange cub who had claimed that he was one of the triplets who were the true Dragon Speakers. Sunset believed he had done it. And the others believed it too, because Ghost had returned with blood on his muzzle—his own, actually—and Pepper had never reappeared. They wouldn't believe that the white monster had actually let Pepper escape into the Northern Forest.

Ghost entered the feast clearing and sighed heavily as he spotted Sunset, lolling under a soft green canopy of bamboo leaves. It was hard even to look at him, let alone take the steps across the clearing to stand at his side.

Ghost didn't understand why the other pandas didn't feel the revulsion he did when they looked at Sunset. They didn't know the depths he'd sunk to, but they certainly knew that Sunset probably knew that Ghost had killed Pepper, and yet he still kept him around, kept giving him work to do.

The title *Dragon Speaker* held so much power. The Dragon

was good—the pandas all knew it, as if they'd been born hold-ing the knowledge—so the Speaker couldn't possibly be bad. Everything he did he must be doing for a good reason.

It was a problem Ghost knew he couldn't solve. They wouldn't believe him if he told them Sunset wasn't a true Dragon Speaker, any more than they had believed Rain when she had tried to tell them. All that would happen would be that Sunset would throw Ghost in the pit with her, or just kill him, whichever was more convenient.

No, he had no choice but to play along for now, even though Sunset had to be stopped, even though he knew that Sunset had manipulated him. He had to play the role of the stupid brute who would do anything for Sunset's approval—in other words, just act exactly like he had before he'd realized any-thing was wrong. He guessed he couldn't blame the other pandas for their blind faith in their leader, when he'd felt the same not so long ago.

*I was so desperate for a place to fit in. I bullied cubs and intimidated monkeys, or tried to. I did everything he said, and I felt great about it. I might have gone further if Shiver hadn't tried to warn me. Now I don't even have her to talk to. And obviously Rain's no help.*

Here in the feast clearing he was surrounded by pandas, bears of his own kind, who he might have called family if things had been different. But he felt more completely alone than he had even when he'd been walking by himself through the mountains, after Winter had died.

He stopped a few bear-lengths from Sunset and shook

himself hard, as if he could shake off the traitorous thoughts before he had to speak to Sunset.

"Dragon Speaker," he said, approaching the reclining bear. "You sent for me." Sunset turned to look at him, and Ghost suddenly realized that he wasn't just relaxing in the shade, as he'd thought. Sunset's brow was furrowed, and he grunted as he sat up.

"Ah, Ghost." He groaned again.

"Is something the matter?" Ghost asked, trying to sound concerned.

"I don't feel quite myself today," Sunset said. "It will pass. But it means I require your help. I'm not up to taking care of this myself."

"Whatever you need," Ghost said.

Sunset sighed, and sat up to lean his back against a patch of bamboo. "There's a pangolin who came to complain to me about her territory." He glanced around at the feast clearing through narrowed eyes. Ghost guessed he was checking who else was in earshot, so he could judge how honest to be with him. He looked over his shoulder and saw that Pebble and Bay were sitting under one of the trees nearby.

"I can't help her, but she doesn't understand that, and now she won't leave my place on the nesting hill. Make her under-stand *for* me, Ghost. Make her leave the Prosperhill and not come back."

*Just like Pepper,* Ghost thought sadly. *You won't tell me to hurt her. It's worse than that—you want me to make that choice all by myself.*

"I don't feel strong enough for another round of arguments," Sunset complained, closing his eyes. "And there'll be no prophecy today. Now leave me." He turned over, with another groan, and showed his hunched back to Ghost.

Ghost sighed and headed for the nesting hill, his head hanging low. He wasn't sure what he would say to this pangolin, but he knew he had to think of something. Sunset had to continue thinking he was a loyal thug.

The pangolin wasn't hard to find. The concerned glances of other pandas led him straight to the nest that she had settled in.

Ghost had never met a pangolin close up before. She was about the size of a red panda, but instead of fur or the leathery skin of a monkey, she had hard scales all over her body. Her back was curved into a hump, and Ghost remembered that pangolins could curl up, as round as the moon, so that their scales protected them from being eaten.

*I bet a panda bite could break that shell,* Ghost thought sadly. *But perhaps if it comes to a fight, she'll curl up and I can just roll her away down the hill. . . .*

The pangolin looked up as he approached. Her small eyes squinted as if she was straining to see who was there, but her long nose twitched and she spoke before Ghost could.

"You, young panda. Have you come to help me get rid of the monkeys?" she asked.

Ghost stopped. Sunset hadn't said anything about monkeys, but he wasn't very surprised to find out that they were involved in this somehow.

"No," he said at last. "I don't think I can do that. But will you tell me what happened?"

"Did His Highness send you?" the pangolin said, wiggling her nose sarcastically.

"Sunset did, yes," Ghost said.

"And he didn't tell you my demands?"

"I'd like to hear them from you." Ghost walked up to the nest and sat down.

The pangolin seemed to consider telling him to get lost. She was hardly fearsome—her armored skin was impressive, but her long claws were clearly built for foraging, not fighting. Still, the way she stood up and hunched her back, making the scales stick up like thorns, made him think that she wouldn't hesitate to give a panda a nasty swipe across the nose.

Then she sat back down again. "Well, I'll tell you what I told the Dragon Speaker. My kin and I have lived on the same hillside for generations. The broken trees make perfect homes for the insects we like to eat, and there's no need to go down into the dark places."

Ghost frowned. Her description sounded very odd. A dark place, with broken trees?

"Earthquakes and floods have come and gone," the pangolin went on, striking the ground with her armored tail for emphasis. "We've weathered storms and driven off marauding manuls. Never needed help from anybody, understand me? And then, three nights ago, the monkeys came. Hundreds of them, it seemed like! They tore through our territory and filled up the trees and scared off or ate half the insects. And when we protested, they told us the Dragon Speaker had granted them the territory, and we could either do what they said or leave. Well, we don't take orders from monkeys, but there were just too many of them to fight. So my kin moved on, and I came here to take it up with the Dragon Speaker. But he denies he told the monkeys they could have the territory, and he won't come and look, or send any other creature to help us."

Ghost took a long breath. He didn't doubt for one moment that she was telling the truth. Was this Sunset's part of the bargain with the monkeys, fulfilled at last? They'd fetched the special bamboo for him, kept Rain and Peony captive, and generally propped up his false reign as Dragon Speaker—and in return, he'd given them territory, and made sure no panda questioned it or stood up for the animals they drove away.

He looked around to make sure that there were no other pandas in earshot, and then he stepped closer to the pangolin and lowered his voice.

"I wish I could help you," he said. She snorted through her long nose, but he pressed on. "Right now, all I can tell you is you're better off finding somewhere to live that's far away from those monkeys. Sunset is lying to you. He did give them your territory. He is not a good Dragon Speaker, and you should stay out of his way, for your own safety."

The pangolin drew back, her front claws pressed together

in front of her. "He . . . he lied?" Her voice was hoarse with shock.

Ghost nodded. "I'm sorry."

"But you work for him. Why do *you* stay here, if it's true that he really is such a bad panda?"

Ghost sighed. "That's a very good question. I wish I had a good answer. Please, just take my word for it. Gather your family and go."

The pangolin hesitated, clacking her claws together anxiously. "All right. I will. But by the Dragon, I hope you're wrong." She trotted out of Sunset's nest and away down the panda path, without looking back.

Ghost stood and watched her go, and thought, *I wish it were that simple for me.*

He started walking too, nervous energy filling his paws. He should report to Sunset, tell him he'd taken care of his pangolin problem, but he couldn't make himself turn toward the feast clearing. Every time he had the chance to double back, he instead pushed on, downhill and away from the other pandas.

*Why do you stay here?*

The pangolin's question echoed in his mind as he walked. Every paw step seemed to press the thought deeper—*why, why, why*—and still no answer came to him. Finally, he found that he'd walked to the edge of the river—to Egg Rocks, which marked the place where it was shallow enough to cross to the other side.

*I could just leave,* he thought. *Take my own advice and go far away from all of this.*

But the land beyond the Northern Forest had rejected him too. He didn't belong in the mountains with the snow leopards any more than he belonged in the Southern Forest with his own kind, who thought he was a dangerous beast.

Perhaps there was somewhere in between, where he could make a home by himself. Perhaps he could even find Shiver again and tell her how sorry he was for not listening to her. All he had to do was walk away from the Southern Forest and not look back.

*But I can't leave.*

He sat down with a huff in a pile of crunchy gingko leaves.

*Why do I stay here? Because I'm the only one who knows the truth about Sunset. I can't just take that truth and walk off into the night with it. I can't abandon the whole Bamboo Kingdom to whatever he and Brawnshanks are planning. I just can't do it.*

Ghost scratched under his chin and gazed across the river, watching a crane wheel overhead, and a pair of golden takins slowly plod over the crossing from the Northern Forest.

He couldn't go on just sabotaging Sunset's orders one by one; he had to help Rain and Peony—however annoying Rain was to talk to—and he had to find a way to expose Sunset that the rest of the pandas would believe.

A splashing sound caught his attention, and he looked up, afraid that one of the takins had slipped and fallen. They were both still upright, but they'd obviously been startled—they were looking at each other and then back at the Northern Forest with wide, fearful eyes. Without a word they scrambled faster over the last few bear-lengths to the southern shore and vanished into the forest, more completely than a pair of lum-bering creatures should be able to.

Ghost hunkered down behind a big rock and peered across at the northern bank.

Something had startled them. Could it be the tiger? He had seen it here before, pacing along the far bank. . . .

The reeds moved, and sure enough, a feline shape slunk out into the river, placing its big paws carefully in the rushing water. But it wasn't the tiger.

*Shiver!*

Ghost's heart felt like it was swelling in his chest. His fur stood on end. It was really her, his littermate, her soft white fur with its gray-brown spots, her fluffy white tail held high so it didn't dangle in the water as she crossed.

He forced himself to wait, pawing the ground in his excite-ment, until she'd made it across the river. Then he scrambled out from behind his rock and pounded down the short slope to Shiver's side. She looked up, her ears pinned back for a moment in surprise, then let out a surprised chirrup as Ghost nuzzled his nose into the soft, damp fur on the side of her face and licked her ear.

"Shiver!" he gasped. "You came back! I'm so glad you came back!"

Shiver rubbed her cheek against his and head-butted his shoulder. "I never left," she said.

"What?" Ghost pulled back to stare into her face.

"Not here. Come on, let's get off the path," Shiver whis-pered, looking warily up at the trees. Ghost let her lead the way into the bushes, too stunned to speak, until she found a hollow just big enough for the two of them at the base of a tree. They curled up together, almost like they had as tiny cubs, and Shiver started to groom the top of Ghost's head as she explained.

"I couldn't just leave," she said. "Not without you. Not without putting an end to Sunset's treachery."

"I'm so sorry I didn't believe you," Ghost sighed. "I should have listened. I just really wanted to think I'd found the place I belonged."

"That doesn't matter now," Shiver said. "You worked it out for yourself. Now all that matters is stopping Sunset. First we have to free his prisoners," she went on. "I've seen them, in that pit, with all the monkeys around them. He thinks he has them completely helpless, but I don't think that's true. They've got me, and you—and Nimbletail."

"Nimbletail?" Ghost frowned. She was one of the younger monkeys, wasn't she?

"I've been watching her—she's not like the others. She'll help us."

Ghost gazed at his sister's determined face with a burning feeling in his throat. This was exactly what he had needed. A plan, a place to begin, an ally—maybe even two.

For the first time since he had figured out that Sunset was up to no good, he felt hope sparkling in his heart like the sun dancing on the river.

# CHAPTER FOUR

RAIN SAT SLUMPED AGAINST the mud wall of the pit, her eyes closed against the dazzling light of High Sun. The trees overhead waved their branches, breaking the sunlight into flickering, sparkling shafts that danced over Rain's face, as if she were looking up at the sun from deep underwater.

She tried to open her eyes, but she couldn't see anything except the slowly shifting light. Everything else around her was darkness, like she was swimming in a deep pool of black water. Her body felt weightless, and she pushed off from the wall and floated up, spiraling through the water. It felt so good to be swimming again, with the soft scattered light playing over her fur. She flipped and rolled, enjoying a freedom she hadn't felt in days.

Then a shape passed overhead. There was no splash, but

now there was something falling through the column of broken light. It was another panda.

It was Sunset.

He descended slowly, but he wasn't swimming, like Rain. He was drowning. His jaws opened in a silent roar of fear, and his claws raked through the black water, looking for something to hold on to.

Rain floated to one side, treading water and watching. She knew that if she reached out to him, his claws would dig into her and she would be dragged down with him.

Even though this was the face of the panda who had tried to drown her, and who had attacked Peony and had them both imprisoned, it was hard to watch Sunset slowly struggle and try to cry out for help as he sank to the bottom of the black pool. And yet she couldn't seem to look away. His eyes were full of fear, and he wore an expression Rain didn't think she had ever seen on Sunset's face before—something like regret.

After what seemed like an awfully long time, Sunset's body went still. It struck the bottom of the black pool and lay there for a moment before the ground seemed to fold over him, wrapping around him like a mother holding her cub. Once he was gone, the ground kept rising, coming closer and closer, in a movement so quick that Rain didn't have time to be afraid before it reached her.

She woke up, slumped against the wall of the pit, blinking in the brilliant High Sun light, and feeling unsteady, as if she'd been falling before a great paw had scooped her up and put her gently back where she'd started.

She got up and shook herself, then looked around, checking that Peony was still dozing on the other side of the pit, squinting up at the sky to see if the white monster or any of the monkeys were watching her. Nobody was paying any attention, and she breathed a sigh of relief. It probably just looked like she'd been napping, but Rain knew that wasn't it at all.

*A vision, finally!*

The Great Dragon had sent her a vision. It hadn't abandoned her. And it had shown her how Sunset would die.

*Perhaps it isn't that literal,* Rain corrected herself. *The Dragon can be tricky like that. But it must mean something! I bet it's the pool.*

That must be the key to defeating him. She needed to find the right place, and get Sunset there somehow.

*Which is good to know,* she added, sagging a little. *But it doesn't help get us out of this pit. . . .*

She loped over to Peony's side and sat down near her, watching her mother's shallow breathing. The movement made Peony stir and open her eyes, but they were crusty, and her focus seemed weak.

"Oh, Rain. What time is it? Did I miss the feast?" She sat up to lean against the mud wall, but it was a slow struggle to get upright.

"It's only a little late," Rain said. She checked the edges of the pit again for prying monkey eyes, and then pulled up the rock where she'd hidden her stashed supplies. They were meager at best. She selected two slightly squashed gingko fruits and a muddy bamboo sprout and pushed them toward Peony.

"I've had mine already," she lied.

Peony probably knew she wasn't telling the truth, but she seemed too weak to argue.

Rain tried to smile as Peony ate, but it was so hard to see her mother suffering like this. Even with Nimbletail throwing down the odd extra bamboo stalk when she could, and Rain making sure Peony got the biggest share of the food, they couldn't go on like this. It hadn't rained today either, which meant that the only water was the half-dried puddle at the very center of the pit.

*It won't be enough. We have to get out of here....*

She reared up on her back legs and planted her front paws on the wall of the pit, listening hard. How many monkeys were up there right now? She couldn't see them, but if she focused, she could hear their chattering voices.

"Hey!" she barked. "We need some more water down here! If you don't want Sunset's hostages dying of thirst, you'd better find a way of getting us some!"

She waited, but there was no reply apart from a soft, derisive snigger.

Being ignored was almost worse than the taunting and stone-throwing that the monkeys had entertained themselves with for the first night and day of their captivity.

She took a deep breath, trying to think of the worst insult she could throw at them. But before she could, she heard several monkey voices calling Brawnshanks's name, as if something was happening that the monkey leader needed to see.

"Brawnshanks, she's back!" one of them chirped.

"Silvermane's back!"

Rain dug her claws into the mud wall of the pit and listened hard as the hubbub died down.

Brawnshanks's voice rose above the rest. "So? Have you taken it?"

"Yes," said a deep female voice. "It is ours at last. It was easy, thanks to the Dragon Speaker."

A chorus of unpleasant monkey giggles filled the clearing.

"We won't need Sunset for much longer," Brawnshanks said.

Rain shuddered. She knew the monkeys were up to something behind Sunset's back. She knew they'd been helping him, and that they were only doing it to get something in return—but she still didn't know what they'd gotten out of the deal.

She held her breath, hoping that the monkeys would talk more about their plans, but then one of her back paws skidded away from her in the mud, and she yelped as she tried to keep her balance.

The monkey voices hushed.

"Hey!" Rain yelled, sitting up quickly and trying to look as if she hadn't been listening at all. "Can you hear me? Is anyone even up there? Maybe I should start climbing out, huh? Anyone? Okay, here I come!"

"What are you going on about now, prisoner?" The familiar large, flat blue face of Brawnshanks himself peered over the edge of the pit.

Rain took a deep breath. She'd been asking for water, but now she looked back at Peony, and her mother's drooping eyelids made her stomach twist and tangle into knots.

"I have a request," she said. "I want you to let Peony out. Sunset won't care; he doesn't need her. She's too weak to stand against Sunset, and it's me he wants."

"Rain, I can't leave you," Peony murmured.

"Yes, you can. You can't stay here, that's for sure. What do you say, Brawnshanks?"

The monkey sat on the edge of the pit and scratched his head, letting his golden tail dangle over the edge.

"Don't see what's in it for me," he sniffed, "Unless you want to give me a prophecy?"

Rain looked down at her paws.

"I can tell you . . ." The words *how Sunset will die* rose at the back of her throat. It would certainly get his attention. But what would happen if she told him that?

She couldn't do it.

She racked her brain for something else, something Brawnshanks would want to know. His deal with Sunset was clearly at some kind of tipping point. She didn't know what their reward had been, but she *did* know that it was the monkeys who'd gathered the stripy bamboo for Sunset. She'd seen them do it. What if . . .

She raised her head. "I saw a great column of rock, deep in the forest. The bamboo that grew there was strange—it was stripy. And I saw it getting sick. It all wilted and died."

"Really?" said Brawnshanks. He leaned over for a moment, examining Rain's face. She tried to remember how to look honest.

Then Brawnshanks threw his head back and laughed.

"Oh, that's perfect!" he crowed. "Thank you, *Dragon Speaker*, but I'm afraid I couldn't care less about your little vision."

Rain frowned at him. "You didn't say it had to help you," she snarled. "I gave you a vision—now let Peony out of here!"

"That was our bargain, wasn't it?" Brawnshanks scratched at his strange flattened nose. "I think . . . no." He grinned and got to his paws.

"We had a deal!" Rain growled.

But Brawnshanks just shook his head and walked out of her sight, still chuckling to himself.

Rain sank down against the pit wall.

She should have known better than to try to make a deal with Brawnshanks. The monkeys didn't give a squished gingko for deals or promises, not when they had all the power.

Peony shuffled over to Rain and laid her chin on Rain's shoulder.

"Thank you for trying," she murmured. "But I won't leave you. Whatever happens, we'll get through it together, all right?"

Rain nodded, and snuggled up to her mother. She gave a

grim smile, despite her anger at the monkeys. If this was what Brawnshanks's promises were really worth, Sunset Deepwood had better watch his back.

They were left alone the rest of that day and into a dry, cloudless night. The moon shone down brightly into the pit, casting half of it in sharp silver light and half in deep black shadow. Rain put her muzzle to the surface of the muddy puddle and then licked her lips carefully, not wanting to waste a drop of moisture. She looked up at the stars glinting through the branches of the trees and tried not to think about water.

*The Dragon wouldn't have sent me that vision about Sunset if it thought we'd never get out of here,* she told herself. *The Dragon knows we'll find a way. I should keep believing it too.*

But right now there was a hole in her heart where that belief should have been. The longer they were trapped here, the weaker they would become, and then even if they could find or make the opportunity to escape, they wouldn't be able to manage it. . . .

A sudden scrabbling noise broke the nighttime silence, and Rain looked up and then jumped to her paws as something big slunk over the edge of the pit and dropped down into the shadows. A pair of slitted eyes opened and blinked at Rain, reflecting the moonlight.

Rain held her breath and tried to bunch her muscles, preparing for a fight, even though she knew she couldn't hope to win in this state.

It was the creature that had been watching them. It stepped out into the moonlight so Rain could see it properly, and she gasped. It moved like Shadowhunter, but it was white with mottled brown spots, and much smaller, with big paws and a long tail that seemed out of proportion to its smaller frame.

Before the creature could attack, or Rain could challenge it, Peony's weak voice emerged from the darkness.

"Shiver? Is that you?"

Rain's mother sat up and staggered over to the feline creature, and to Rain's bewilderment, the creature sat and pressed her head gently against Peony's.

"It's me," she said.

"What?" Rain hissed.

"Are you all right, dear?" Peony asked the creature, looking up at the edge of the pit. "Will you be able to get out?"

"Oh yes," the cat replied. "I can leap out of here, no problem."

"Mother? What is happening?" Rain hissed again.

"I'm sorry, Rain," Peony said. "This is Shiver. She's a snow-leopard cub."

"I can see that," Rain huffed. "What's she doing this far from the mountains?"

"That's a long story," said the leopard. She tucked her fluffy tail around her big paws and nodded to Rain in greeting. "You must be Rain. It's nice to finally meet you."

"Shiver is Ghost's littermate," Peony said.

Rain stared at her and then at Shiver, but their expressions remained softly neutral, as if Peony *hadn't* just said something totally bizarre.

"You're aware that Ghost is a bear, right?" she said at last. "And also, he's working for Sunset! If she's his sister, how do we know she's not here to finish us off?"

"That's a long story too," Shiver said. "And we don't have time for it right now. Ghost's not who you think he is."

Rain shook her head. "I'm supposed to believe that? Why hasn't he helped us, if he's on our side?"

"We are helping you," said a growly voice from above her head. She scrambled around to look, and there was Ghost, his white fur glowing, lit from behind by the bright moon over his shoulder. "If you'll just listen to us."

His face disappeared for a moment, and there was a soft rustling, and then a long, beautiful bamboo cane was pushed over the edge and down into the pit. Then another. They were four times as long as the pitiful sprouts they'd been fed for the last few days, and thick with delicious-looking leaves.

"Thank you, Ghost!" Peony whispered. "See, Rain? They're here to help us! The Great Dragon must have sent them."

Rain stared up at Ghost's strange white face.

*Did the Dragon send you?* she wondered. *If this is a trick, it's an elaborate one . . . and in any case, what else am I going to do with my time? Sit here and starve? Whatever they have planned, it's got to be better than that.*

"All right," she said. "So what's the plan?"

# CHAPTER FIVE

GHOST PAWED THE GROUND impatiently, dragging his claws through the soft earth as he listened to Blossom and Ginseng fussing over Sunset.

"You must eat something, Dragon Speaker," said Blossom, nosing the pile of bamboo closer to Sunset.

Sunset let out a harrumph and kicked it away.

Ghost watched and winced as the scar on Sunset's flank stretched as he moved. Whatever was wrong with Sunset, it was obviously real—the sicker he felt, the more the scar seemed inflamed and sore. It was a horrible swollen pink now.

*We've got to get out of here,* he thought. But the plan couldn't go ahead without Nimbletail, and so for now he was stuck here, trying not to do anything to make Sunset—or his thuggish followers—suspicious of him.

"Go," Sunset snapped at Blossom. "You two are doing me no good, hovering like that. Go and make sure those lazy pandas are doing their duties. Ghost, you stay."

Blossom snorted in Ghost's face as she and Ginseng stomped past him, but Ghost refused to flinch. She was a bully, and he wasn't surprised she'd allied herself so closely with Sunset.

"Ghost, come." Sunset gestured with one paw, and winced as he turned over to look at Ghost. "Tell me about the pangolin. I assume you handled it."

"Yes, Dragon Speaker," Ghost said. "She left. She won't cause you any more problems."

"Are you certain?" Sunset said, narrowing his eyes.

"I convinced her that staying here wouldn't be in her best interest," Ghost answered plainly. It was the exact truth, and it grated against his teeth as he watched Sunset consider it and then nod. Did the Dragon Speaker think he'd intimidated the pangolin? Attacked her? Worse? It wasn't clear, but either way, he clearly considered the problem dealt with.

"Good. Listen to me, Ghost. With Pepper gone, and Rain where she is, the triplets pose less of a threat. But one is still out there, unaccounted for, and they will still be able to cause problems. With me indisposed like this, it's all the more vital that you find the last triplet and make sure they never threaten us."

"I will," Ghost lied. He touched his nose gently to Sunset's paw. He tried to remember that Sunset thought he was a useful idiot, not a schemer like Blossom; that was why he trusted him with more of his plans than the others. Ghost had to keep that going, just for a few more days. . . .

"Nothing will stand in your way, I promise," he told Sunset, putting as much earnestness into his voice as he could. "Once they're all dealt with, the threat to the Bamboo Kingdom will be over, and we can all go back to living together peacefully."

"That's right," said Sunset. "Until I get better, I need you out there, looking for the last triplet. That's a direct order."

"Yes, Dragon Speaker." Ghost bowed low, crouching to touch his muzzle to the ground.

"Yes, why don't you go and do that?" said a voice, and Ghost looked up into the tree above his head. He was annoyed, but not that surprised, to see Brawnshanks sitting in the branches, dangling his back legs casually.

How long had he been there? Ghost knew it didn't matter—Brawnshanks must know all about Sunset's plans. But he pretended to be angry, and snarled up at the golden monkey.

"Don't creep up on the Dragon Speaker like that! He's not feeling well—he needs his rest, not monkeys jumping out of trees at him!"

"It's all right, Ghost," Sunset said weakly. "What do you want, Brawnshanks?"

"Nothing, except to help you out," said Brawnshanks. "I've got some *very* interesting news. For your ears only. Run along, Snowy." He waggled his fingers dismissively at Ghost. Ghost pulled a face at him and looked at Sunset, who turned to him and nodded.

"Go on. You have your orders. I wish to talk to Brawn-shanks alone."

Trying not to look as relieved as he felt to be getting out of Sunset's presence, Ghost bowed again and walked away.

He paused as he left the feast clearing and turned the corner, out of sight of Sunset and Brawnshanks. Perhaps he ought to creep around through the undergrowth, so he could listen in and hear what kind of news the monkey leader would call "very interesting"? But he shook himself. He'd probably be caught, and in any case, there was something else he needed to do.

He and Shiver found Nimbletail waiting where they'd agreed, sitting on a high rock in an isolated part of the forest. Nimble-tail tapped nervously on the surface of the rock with the seed from inside a gingko fruit.

"You're late," she said. "It's almost High Sun. I can't be here long. If Brawnshanks hears about this . . ."

"Brawnshanks is with Sunset," Ghost told her. "It's all right."

Nimbletail put down the seed, but she started playing with her tail instead, twisting and curling it between her lithe fin-gers. "I'm sorry about him," she said. "I'm sorry about your friends in the pit. I'm sorry about everything!"

"It's not your fault," Shiver reassured her.

Ghost knew they didn't have very long, and they needed to talk about the escape plan, but he couldn't stop himself from asking, "Do you know what Brawnshanks is planning? Why has he been helping Sunset? What does he get out of it?"

Nimbletail frowned. "I don't know much. My mother says things used to be different. Before the flood, we were content to rule the treetops and eat and play—well, and fight, but only with each other! Now Brawnshanks is always planning. He's obsessed with getting control over the Broken Forest—he says it's where monkeys used to live long ago or something? I don't understand why it means we've got to keep pandas captive."

Shiver looked at Ghost with a confused tilt of her head, but the name "Broken Forest" reminded Ghost of something. What was it the pangolin had said about a dark place with broken trees . . . ?

"Thank you for helping us," Shiver said.

Nimbletail nodded. "Of course. But look, I do have a condition. If Brawnshanks ever finds out I helped you, I'm *dead*. So if I help you get them out, you have to take them and leave the Southern Forest and never come back."

"Agreed," said Shiver. "We want to be as far away from Sunset as we can."

Ghost felt a pang of uncertainty. Sure, he'd love to take his sister and the others and leave, and they'd probably be more likely to find a way to defeat Sunset without living right under his nose. But what about Pebble, and the cubs, and all the other pandas? What would happen to them, left alone with an angry Dragon Speaker?

But he didn't contradict Shiver. They needed this plan to work, and they needed Nimbletail.

"All right," the monkey said, smoothing out the fur on her tail. "What do you need me to do?"

"It'll be tomorrow night," Ghost said. "It's a new moon, so it'll be extra dark. Shiver will sneak in again tonight and make sure the others are ready. And then you run in. . . ."

Ghost managed to avoid Sunset, and most of the other pandas, for almost the rest of the day. He skipped some feasts, and lurked at the edge of the clearing during others. He didn't want to find himself caught up in any more of Sunset's schemes, and he didn't care if the pandas saw him and thought he was being creepy.

At least, he thought he didn't care. But when the time came to settle down to sleep after the Feast of Dying Light, he rolled over to say good night to Pebble in the next nest, and saw the young bear dragging his pile of soft moss farther away. Pebble obviously thought Ghost was asleep, and when he turned to check, Ghost quickly laid his head down and mostly closed his eyes. He watched through the slits, his heart sinking as Pebble picked up mouthfuls of the moss and moved them around a bamboo clump, out of sight of Ghost's own sleeping place.

*Why now?* Ghost thought miserably. *My company was good enough for you before.*

It didn't matter. Soon he'd be gone. All that mattered was getting Rain and Peony out.

He curled up into a ball, as tight as he could, and tried to sleep.

* * *

The following morning, Ghost knew he couldn't avoid Sunset all day, so he went to him after the Feast of Gray Light. The Dragon Speaker was standing again now, and eating with the other pandas. He moved around with only a hint of slowness to show how unwell he'd been the day before. Ghost was horrified to realize that he felt a little relieved.

"You look better today, Dragon Speaker," he said.

"Yes," growled Sunset. "And I know why. I didn't eat a thing yesterday. The sickness was in the bamboo!"

Ghost cast a horrified look at the pile of shredded bamboo stalks nearby.

"Not that bamboo," Sunset snapped. "The striped bamboo. *Brawnshanks*," he spat. "He's swapped the normal type for something that's diseased. He poisoned me, that old liar! And I won't stand for it. Come with me, Ghost. I may need you." And with that, Sunset stalked out of the clearing and headed into the forest.

Ghost hurried after him, his mind spinning. Could Sunset be mistaken? Or was Brawnshanks actually trying to kill the Dragon Speaker? Was that somehow part of his plan? What if Sunset was leading him toward a confrontation he couldn't get out of?

They pushed through creaking stands of bamboo and clambered down steep slopes, Sunset taking the shortest route to the monkeys' territory. He seemed to be propelled by his anger, continuing on even as Ghost could hear the breath rasping in his throat.

They burst into a clearing where a group of monkeys were sitting on the ground, seemingly playing with rocks, moving them around. Several of them squeaked in alarm and leaped up into the trees, but Brawnshanks stood his ground as Sunset stomped toward him, as did an older monkey and a younger one. They flanked their leader with determined expressions on their squashed blue faces.

"Dragon Speaker," said Brawnshanks. "What can I do for you? You're looking well—or are you? If you're tired from the walk down from your perch, you can sit."

Sunset blew several heavy, labored breaths from his nostrils. The fur on Brawnshanks's head stirred, but the monkey didn't move a muscle. Ghost sidestepped so that he could watch the monkeys.

*But if it came to a fight between these two, whose side would I be on?*

"I know what you did," Sunset growled. "If I'm looking well, it's because I stopped eating that poisoned bamboo you've been giving me."

"*Poisoned?*" Brawnshanks almost fell down in exaggerated shock. "I wouldn't do such a thing."

He might as well have said *yes, I poisoned you, you stupid panda.* Ghost knew now without a doubt that he had done it, and Sunset obviously did too. Sunset let out a furious roar, spittle flying from his jaws as he opened them wider and wider, almost enough to swallow Brawnshanks whole. His voice was deep and gravelly as he shouted into Brawnshanks's face, "I'm the Dragon Speaker here! You monkeys are supposed to be working for me!"

Brawnshanks froze for a moment. Then he sat up straight, the innocent fainting act forgotten. Ghost felt a shudder run all the way down his back underneath his fur as the monkey looked the huge, furious panda right in the eye.

"You're not the one in charge here . . . *Sunset*," he said, putting a long and tense pause before Sunset's name.

Ghost looked from Brawnshanks's calm face to Sunset's furious one and back, but before he could figure out just what Brawnshanks meant, the monkey went on.

"You are a deluded fraud and nothing more. The monkeys have taken the Broken Forest, with your invaluable help. And now you will go back to your faithful followers, and you will make sure that we keep it. If not, perhaps I'll have something to say to them about Sunset Deepwood and whether or not he's the true Dragon Speaker. Eh?"

Ghost's prickling skin twitched at this, and he instinctively took a step back. Was this confirmation from Brawnshanks? Was Sunset really lying to them all about everything?

Sunset didn't seem to notice that Ghost had moved. He was staring at Brawnshanks as if he wanted to rip his throat out right then and there.

"And of course," Brawnshanks said, "if anything should happen to me, then Silvermane or Jitterpaws here, or any number of other monkeys, will be along to tell the story instead of me." The younger monkey beside him crouched as if she was ready to spring into the trees, while the older, silver-furred one stared coldly into Sunset's eyes. "And maybe they'll have even more stories to tell—about foolish pandas who believe they get visions from ordinary striped bamboo. And about what really happened to Plum Slenderwood."

Ghost stood by silently, not daring to breathe. He couldn't imagine Sunset backing down—the big panda's whole body was shaking with rage, his sides heaving as his breath came heavier and heavier.

"The monkeys in the Broken Forest," Brawnshanks said, his voice turning weirdly gentle, almost singsong, "and Sunset Deepwood in his rightful place at the head of his devoted, faithful pandas. That's how it's meant to be. Let's not do anything to ruin it, shall we, my friend?"

Ghost's throat was dry, but he couldn't bring himself to swallow in case it shattered the silence that fell between Sunset and Brawnshanks. It felt as if the air were stretched thin, like skin over a broken bone.

Brawnshanks moved first, stepping away, motioning for the other two monkeys to follow him. They turned and walked from the clearing, showing their backs to Sunset in a way that Ghost thought was deeply risky. But Sunset didn't move until they were gone.

Ghost took another few small steps back, away from Sunset, trying to move as slowly and quietly as he could. Fear gripped him, and he wondered if he should run, or say something, but neither path seemed to end anywhere but with Sunset's teeth in Ghost's throat.

The Dragon Speaker was shaking all over. He sat down on

his haunches and stared for a moment at the pebbles that the monkeys had been playing with when they'd arrived. Then he let out a mighty roar that startled birds from the trees, and slapped the pebbles away with one claw, scattering them across the clearing. Silence fell again, broken only by Sunset's heavy breathing, before he let out another roar, this one longer and more tortured. He screamed with rage and lashed out at the nearest tree, raking his claws against it again and again until the bark was ragged and splintered.

Ghost backed up more and more, until he reached the edge of the clearing. Sunset was still roaring, cursing Brawnshanks and all his kind, and attacking the tree as if he wanted to bring it down.

Ghost slipped away into the forest, as fast as he could without drawing attention to himself. He walked, heart hammering in his throat, changing direction at random until he was pretty sure Sunset wouldn't be able to follow.

Sunset might be angry with him later. But this was better than facing him now, away from the others, with his slavering jaws and his eyes full of rage. He'd been beaten by the monkeys without them ever laying a finger on him.

*What will he do now?*

Ghost had considered simply hiding from all the pandas until night fell, and possibly never seeing Sunset again. But he wanted to know what the Dragon Speaker would do. It might change the escape plan—it might change *everything.*

So he climbed the hill to the clearing for the Feast of Long Light, with all the other pandas, though they kept their distance. He thought some of them were shunning him even more openly now, slowing their pace so that they could walk far behind him. He had seen the parents of the group steer their cubs away from him before, but now Cypress and Horizon bodily moved Fir out of his line of sight and stood in front of her, glaring at him as he passed.

Sunset was already in the feast clearing, flanked by Blossom and Ginseng, when Ghost reached the top of the hill. Their eyes met, and Ghost saw a flash of some emotion he couldn't identify cross Sunset's face—was it annoyance at Ghost for leaving, or more like shame for the way he'd lost control? Ghost padded close to him and bowed.

"I'm sorry I left earlier, Dragon Speaker," he said. "I . . . I was a coward."

He looked up slowly, and saw Sunset regarding him with a frown.

"You're forgiven," he said. He looked like he might be about to say more but then thought better of it. He turned instead, shaking out his fur, and climbed up into the low branches of the tree where he liked to sit while he listened for the Great Dragon's messages.

Brawnshanks's words echoed through Ghost's mind.

*A deluded fraud, and nothing more . . . something to say about whether Sunset Deepwood is the true Dragon Speaker . . .*

He shuddered. He knew that Sunset wasn't all he said he

was, and Rain had *told* him that the Dragon Speaker was a liar and a fraud . . . but somehow it hadn't quite sunk in until now, when he was watching Sunset climb into the tree, clutching the blue stone. The pandas' faces were turned upward, their eyes full of innocence and expectation. Ghost saw Frog and Maple lying on their bellies side by side, their heads on their paws and eyes wide. They trusted him completely. And he was about to lie to them all.

Sunset closed his eyes and tipped his head back, holding the stone out in front of him. Ghost squinted at it. Was it anything but an ordinary rock? It certainly was very blue, and it seemed to glimmer strangely in the light, even though Ghost was sure there was no power or connection to any Dragon running through it. Where had Sunset gotten it?

Sunset opened his eyes with a gasp. The collected pandas mirrored him with their own intake of breath.

"My friends, the Dragon has spoken to me," he said.

Ghost braced himself. *Will he tell us the Dragon wants the pandas to go to war with the monkeys? Or undermine Brawnshanks somehow?*

"The Dragon is kind and generous, not just to its faithful pandas, but to all the creatures in the kingdom," Sunset went on. "I have seen a great forest of broken trees, and our friends the golden-haired monkeys living there peacefully. That territory was theirs, once, and the Dragon wishes it to be so again. The monkeys have returned to their home. It is the duty of every panda to help make sure they can remain there safely."

Ghost turned slowly to look at the other pandas. Some were

nodding sagely; others turned and muttered to each other. But none of them questioned Sunset's prophecy.

The Dragon Speaker climbed down and took hold of one of the long bamboo canes, holding it in front of him and speaking the blessing for the Feast of Long Light. Ghost watched silently as he thanked the Dragon for its gift of endurance, and then as all the pandas picked up their feasts and the clearing filled with the splintering of bamboo.

*He gave Brawnshanks everything he asked for,* Ghost thought. *He's doing exactly as he was told. So everything Brawnshanks said . . . it's all true.* The monkey leader could destroy Sunset, that much was clear. But instead he had chosen to leave him as Dragon Speaker. *And that's because Brawnshanks can use him to make all of the Bamboo Kingdom believe whatever he wants.*

At the end of the feast, Ghost wanted to slip away, but Sunset called his name and gestured for him to follow him to the secluded spot where Sunset slept during the day and held court with his loyal thugs. Ghost couldn't refuse him, not in front of the others, but his paws felt like heavy stones as he padded across the clearing and around the high rock. He didn't like leaving the view of the other pandas one bit. He only hoped that if Sunset attacked him, he would be able to roar for help loudly enough to be heard. . . .

Sunset was waiting for him behind the rock. Ghost approached, then stopped, hanging his head. "Yes, Dragon Speaker?"

"I've told three of the monkeys to go and deal with some

flying squirrels that are causing trouble in the Northern Forest, near their precious new territory."

Ghost blinked at this. "Um, yes? What did the squirrels
do?"

"Nothing—there are no squirrels," snapped Sunset.

". . . what?"

"It's a lie. You understand what that is, right?" Sunset
sneered. "I want you to go with the monkeys to the Northern Forest and kill them. That'll show Brawnshanks who
he's dealing with. Show him I'm . . ." He trailed off, staring
at Ghost with a dark, exhausted look on his large face. "The
monkeys are waiting outside the clearing. Just go."

Ghost hesitated. There was a high ringing sound in his
ears. A direct order to murder unsuspecting creatures, for no
reason but Sunset's pride!

Then he saw Sunset's lip curl into a snarl. "Yes, Dragon
Speaker," he said. "At once."

He backed away, bowing as he went.

Sure enough, three monkeys were waiting for him at the
edge of the clearing. They were talking to Yew and Mist.
Ghost imagined that the pandas must be asking about the
Broken Forest.

Two of the monkeys he didn't know, but one of them was
Jitterpaws, the younger of the two followers who had been
there at the clearing when Brawnshanks had ripped Sunset's
pride to shreds.

*I can't do this,* Ghost thought, even as he kept walking across the feast clearing, even as he exchanged a knowing nod with Jitterpaws and they headed out toward the river. *I won't murder these monkeys on Sunset's say-so. But I've got to do something—the escape is happening tonight! I have to shake them off and get back here by Moon Climb.* . . .

# CHAPTER SIX

NIGHT CAME, AND IT was so dark that Rain could barely make out the white of Peony's fur right beside her in the pit, even though their shoulders were touching. Just as Shiver had said, no moon had risen tonight. The clearing was quiet, with just a few short mutterings from the monkey guards and the occasional sound of chewing to break the tense silence that seemed to fill up the pit like the black water from Rain's vision.

She could feel Peony's shoulders trembling with every breath.

"What if we're caught?" she whispered, close to Rain's ear.

"We'll be fine," Rain whispered back. "We've got help. They all know what they're doing. It's going to be fine."

*Do they, though? Is it going to be fine?* Rain's thoughts put in. She tried to push them down. *You're not helping! If it all goes wrong . . . well, we'll deal with it then.*

"Hey!" came a high squeal. Peony jumped, and Rain herself let out a startled yip. "Hey, you! You have to come!"

"Who's there?" cried one of the monkey guards.

"It's me, Nimbletail!"

Rain glanced at Peony, and they pressed together, listening hard—though none of the monkeys were speaking in whispers now. Nimbletail seemed to be pausing to take several big, gasping breaths, as if she'd run all the way here.

"It's—it's—the forest! The Broken Forest!"

"What?" one of the other monkeys demanded. "What in all the kingdoms are you talking about?"

"Brawnshanks," Nimbletail gasped. "He says to come. Sent me to get every monkey I could find. The Northern Forest pandas won't listen to Sunset; they're going to invade, take back the Broken Forest! We've gotta go!"

"Those big stupid bears," one of the other monkeys growled. "C'mon, we'll show them whose territory that forest is!"

"Hang on," said another. "The prisoners—we shouldn't just leave them."

Rain held her breath, pulling back the groan of disappointment building in her chest. What would they do if the monkeys refused to leave?

"Brawnshanks said *every* monkey," Nimbletail said. "What do I tell him?"

There was a pause.

"They'll never get out of there by themselves," said one of the others. "C'mon."

Rain pressed her shoulder to Peony's and allowed herself to breathe, careful not to make any sound louder than the scuffles and whoops from up above. She listened to the sounds of branches creaking, imagined small paws rushing up bark and through the canopy, the sounds fading and fading. . . .

Were they gone? A few small noises persisted, but it was just the wind in the trees, mice rustling in the undergrowth. She was almost certain.

"It's time," said Peony. "They could come back at any moment. We have to go."

Rain stretched out, feeling her tense muscles crunch and pull across her back. Peony was right. Even if they'd left one monkey behind, this was the best opportunity they would ever get.

"Where are those paw holds?" Peony muttered. In the darkness Rain sensed rather than saw her going to the side of the pit and sniffing at the packed earth. "Here's one, I think . . . yes, here's the next. This is it."

Rain knew she was right. She'd spent all day staring at the holes in the wall of the pit that Shiver had dug the night before, after she'd used her feline stealth to creep past the dozing monkey guards. Rain had tried to commit the pattern of paw holds to memory, so that when she had to use them in the pitch dark, she would have some idea where to reach next. She hoped that memory would help her now.

Rain reared up on her back legs, put her paws into the first paw holds, and began to pull herself up, nose to the muddy earth.

*Our mother did the same for Ghost once,* Shiver had said. Rain still didn't really understand how Shiver and Ghost could have the same mother, but Shiver had told a story as she'd worked to scratch out the earth, finding the safest way, using the biggest rocks and tree roots as a path to the top. She'd said that in the mountains Ghost had once fallen into a deep chasm called the Endless Maw, and their mother—the snow leopard Winter—had found the way down to his ledge and shown him how to climb out.

Rain pushed herself up with her back legs, reaching with her front right paw, feeling for the hole she knew ought to be there. She couldn't find it. Her heart dropped with fear, as if there were a howling, snowy abyss below her too. But then her claws caught something and she reached with all her might until she got a paw over the lip of a tree root and into the next paw hold. She almost had to swing on her claws to pull herself up.

*Wherever Leaf is right now,* she thought, *I wish we could swap places. She'd be up out of this pit in a heartbeat.*

The thought of her sister led her to remember how they had parted—with Leaf off to chase a sign from the Dragon, which Rain thought was foolishness, and Rain lying to her, promising to stay with Plum and find the other Northern Forest pandas.

*I have to find her again. I need to tell her I'm sorry. . . .*

Rain felt strength flow into her paws as she reached for the next paw hold, and the next. Then, all of a sudden, she felt clear air where she expected earth, and her claws dug into clumps of grass and fallen leaves. She heaved herself up and over and flopped down onto the smooth ground, a sigh of relief bursting from her chest as she rolled over and looked around the clearing. Out here, the darkness seemed less deep than it had been in the pit, and her eyes could adjust better. She could make out the space, the shapes of tree trunks, the pattern of branches against the stars.

No monkeys. Nobody was watching them.

Rain staggered to her paws and stomped on the spot for a moment, shaking out her fur. She was free!

"It's all right," she called down into the pit. "They're really gone. You can do it," she added. She could just make out Peony's white fur moving against the dark earth wall of the pit. She had already started the climb. Rain's heart climbed with her, up into Rain's throat, as her mother's weak limbs shook and she paused to catch her breath. But Peony never wavered, though Rain could see and hear the effort she was making. Rain moved over and went right up to the edge, leaning her head and shoulders over. As soon as Peony was within grabbing distance, she seized the scruff of her neck in her teeth, just as Peony had done to Rain when she was a little cub, and pulled her mother up and over the edge.

Peony collapsed in a heap, trembling and gasping, but alive—and *free*.

"We made it," Rain panted.

"I hope . . . ," Peony began, then paused as she gathered her strength and pushed herself up onto her paws with a big huffing sound, swaying just a little. "I hope we see Shiver again soon. I hope she knows how grateful we are."

"We will," Rain said. "She'll find us after we meet Ghost by the river. Can you walk? We have to get out of here."

"I'm fine," Peony said.

Their paws squelched on the ground as they walked across the clearing. The whole place smelled strongly of monkey, littered with the mess of the guards and the old fruit they'd left dropped on the ground. Rain half hoped that it might mask their scent, so that even if any pandas were wandering the forest, they might not be noticed.

Outside the clearing, Rain stopped and scented the air. She felt disoriented, as if the world outside the pit had been spun around while they were down there. She didn't remember which way the monkeys had marched them from the panda path, or which way they should go to the river.

"Downhill," she muttered. "If in doubt, head downhill."

She tried to scent around her for anything familiar, as they picked their way through ferns and over the rocks. She smelled the mingled scents of creatures and bamboo, and her stomach grumbled at her, but they couldn't stop to eat—they couldn't risk the time or the noise.

Then, finally, the ground underfoot felt smoother, with ferns and grass that had been trodden down over years, and a strong scent of pandas. The panda path! All of a sudden, the smells and dim shapes came together, and Rain knew exactly where she was. She had walked this path all her life, and she knew where it led—to the river.

"Come on!" she whispered to Peony. "It's not far now!"

The path wound down the hill, around rocks, and between trees. At the river, Ghost would meet them, and then they'd just have to cross the water—hard, with Peony so weak, but not impossible—and then they could disappear into the Northern Forest, and they'd be safe to regroup, to find Leaf, to plan Sunset's downfall. . . .

Rain turned a corner, and only after she'd taken a few steps did she realize what she was seeing, and her heart skipped several beats.

There was a panda on the path, sitting, looking toward her. Watching her.

Rain stumbled to a halt, and bunched her muscles to run, either away or into a fight if the panda was one of Sunset's thugs. . . .

"Rain," said the panda, and she gasped.

"Pebble!"

She almost started forward to press her head to his in greeting, but then she stopped herself. Pebble hadn't helped her when she'd come to face Sunset. When she'd said he was false, and had tried to drown her, not one of the Prosperhill pandas had believed her—not even Pebble.

"Please," she whispered. "You have to help us. We just want to leave the Southern Forest. That's all. You can think I'm a liar if you want. Just let me go."

"Rain, I . . ." Pebble's voice was croaky, as if he was having to force the words out. He shook his head. "I don't know what to do. The Dragon Speaker needs me."

"The Dra—" Rain cut herself off. She wouldn't call him that. "Pebble, look at my mother. She's weak. He's been *starving* her. He was keeping us in a *pit*, having the monkeys stand guard night and day."

"He said that he would kill me if Rain didn't cooperate," said Peony in a low voice. "Please, dear Pebble. If you won't help us, just turn your back and let us pass."

Rain watched Pebble in the darkness. He didn't move a muscle. He didn't react at all to hearing that his best friend and her mother had been kept prisoner by his Dragon Speaker.

"You knew," she said. "Maybe you *all* knew, or maybe just you—maybe he's told you you're *special*? Maybe he's said he trusts you so much that he knows he can tell you about the hard choices he's had to make?"

Now Pebble's shoulders and head drooped, and she got the impression, even in the dark, that he was trying not to look at her.

"That's the kind of thing Sunset said to me, too," Rain pressed. "Right before he tried to *drown* me!"

Pebble started shaking his head and backing away. "I—I can't believe that," he muttered. "I just can't. . . ."

Too late, Rain realized she'd pushed too hard.

"They're here!" Pebble cried. "Rain and Peony! They're escaping!"

Anger flared in Rain's chest and she ran straight at Pebble. She caught him off guard and managed to barge right into him, knocking him off the path.

"Run!" she shouted to Peony. As her mother rushed past her, she paused, leaning down to bare her teeth at Pebble. "If Peony gets hurt, I will *never* forgive you," she whispered. "Get a grip, idiot. It might already be too late."

Then she turned and ran.

She could already hear the sounds of cracking bamboo stems and large paws striking the earth behind them. She led Peony on a shortcut, leaving the path and scrambling down an almost-sheer slope, hoping to shake them off for long enough to get to the river. In the dark her paws struck rocks and made her stumble. Peony's breath was rasping, and her steps were slowing.

*Dragon, let Ghost have heard the racket too,* Rain thought.

The bamboo along the path shook, and then, with an almighty crack, a large panda shape crashed through the canes, right into Peony, bowling her over onto her side and standing over her, growling. It was Blossom. Rain roared and launched herself at the horrible panda, biting down hard on her ear and pulling. Blossom yelped and reared back, trying to shake Rain off. Peony scrambled unsteadily to her paws.

"Run!" Rain yelled through a mouthful of Blossom's fur. She could already hear more stomping paws behind her, coming down the path. But Peony didn't run. She reared back and aimed a swipe at Blossom's face. Blossom yelped again and staggered, and Rain dug her claws into the back of Blossom's neck and then slid off her back. Perhaps they could be gone before—

Sunset and Ginseng pounded into view. "Stop them!" Sunset cried. "Kill them!"

Rain barely had time to think before Ginseng was on her and she was trapped between him and the groaning Blossom. Ginseng's open jaws came right at her head, and she had to throw herself to the ground to keep out of his way. His teeth snapped at the back of her neck and she felt a few hairs tug out as she rolled away.

Blossom was facing off with Peony now, baring her teeth as Peony backed away on trembling paws. Rain felt something grab her by the scruff and pull her back, and she tried to turn and lash out, but Ginseng shook her hard, then threw her down to the ground again.

*Where is Ghost?* Rain thought desperately, dazed. *He said that if it came to a fight, he would help us. . . .*

Then Sunset was looming over her, his eyes glinting in the darkness. She tried to scramble away, but he brought both his front paws down, and it was all she could do to turn so that his long, sharp claws only grazed her flank, instead of raking her across the belly.

She winced as hot, throbbing pain spread across her side, but swallowed any sound. She had to get to Peony, had to get out of here. Three large, well-fed, ruthless pandas against two weak and starving ones. They had to run. If they fought, they would die.

She scrambled off the path and into a patch of ferns as if she were diving into the deep river. Sunset roared, and she felt the ferns stir and shake as one of the pandas shoved through them, searching for her, but she was already gone, pushing through and back out onto the path, on the other side of Blossom, in time to leap between her and Peony.

Blossom's teeth caught Rain's ear. Rain felt it tear as Blossom tried to yank her aside, and *then* she felt the pain, sharp and deep, as if Blossom's teeth had bitten her right in the side of the head. She felt a hot trickle of blood run into her fur.

"Run, now!" she yelled. Then she and Peony were off again. Behind them she heard shouts and crackling as Sunset and Ginseng pulled themselves out of the ferns, and the sound of Blossom's roar, and then Rain could actually feel the ground beneath her paws shake as all three pandas started to run after them.

*We can't do this,* she thought, before a white shape stepped out onto the path in front of her. It wasn't Ghost—it was Shiver.

"This way!" Shiver hissed, and leaped from the path into the undergrowth, slipping through a gap between a tree and a bamboo stand.

*Will we be able to follow where a leopard goes?* Rain wondered, but when she came to the gap, she threw herself at it, and made it through. She paused just long enough to see that Peony was with her, then turned and chased after the swishing, fluffy white blur that was Shiver's tail. It led them on a winding trail that wove down a steep hill through the bushes and around trees, but always through spaces just big enough for a panda to squeeze through that Rain knew she wouldn't have spotted in the dark.

"I smell them! This way!" growled Ginseng from somewhere behind them. There was a loud cracking as one of the other pandas barged straight into the bamboo, forcing their way through.

For the first time since she'd seen Pebble, Rain felt a flash of hope. Could they really lose Sunset like this?

But no—they were afraid, and she was bleeding; they must be leaving a trail, and it wouldn't be long before they had to slow down, or they would fall down—

Then, suddenly, her paws splashed into cold water. She skidded instinctively to a halt, and Peony stumbled into her from behind. Where were they? This wasn't the river; there was still thick foliage on every side. . . .

"Keep going," hissed Shiver, padding back toward them. "But walk in the stream—it'll help hide your scent!"

Rain nodded fiercely, uncertain if the leopard could even see her in this darkness, and hurried forward into the stream. The water was freezing, and it wasn't a quiet way to move, but she could still hear the crunching of bamboo canes and Sunset growling at his two thugs from somewhere up the slope. They were making so much noise, it covered the splashing of six pairs of paws as Shiver, Rain, and Peony hurried down through tunnels of ferns and bushes. And then, all at once, the ferns opened up and Rain saw the river. The faint light of the stars seemed almost as bright as the moon out here, and she saw the glint on the broken surface of the water, and wished she could dive right in and swim to safety. But Peony stumbled to a halt beside Rain and leaned on her, and every muscle in her body seemed to be trembling.

"We're not far from Egg Rocks," whispered Shiver. "Let's go!"

Sure enough, they didn't have to walk much farther before the large, rounded rocks loomed out of the dark in front of them. Rain let Peony go first, so she could watch for any sign she might fall and be swept into the deeper part of the river. The cold water lapped against the scratches on her side, and she shuddered, but she forced herself to keep on walking, her legs stiff with pain and exhaustion, until they had both safely made it to the far bank.

Shiver led the way into the Northern Forest until they were deep in the shadow of the trees, where even in the daylight Sunset wouldn't be able to see them from the Southern Forest.

Then both Rain and Peony sank down onto their bellies, gasping for breath. Peony was still shaking, and without a word Shiver came close and tucked her thick white tail around her.

"Thank you," Rain said, when she could hear again over the sound of her pounding heart. "But what happened to Ghost? He was supposed to be there to help us!"

"I don't know," Shiver said. She hung her head miserably. "I can't find him anywhere."

Rain huffed and got to her paws. "So he left us in the lurch? What, did he decide he'd be better off on his own? Or maybe he's picked Sunset after all!"

"No! I'm sure . . . I'm sure there must be a good explanation," Shiver said. Her tail twitched. "I'm sure he didn't mean to."

Rain snorted. She went over to Peony and nudged her gently to her paws. "C'mon. We've got to keep moving. And clearly we can't wait for Ghost. We should never have trusted him."

Shiver growled just a little, her tail twitching as she uncurled it from around Peony's shoulders. "Hey. I promise you, Ghost is on our side. I just don't know where he is right now. . . ."

Rain turned on her.

"Well, we made it—but it was no thanks to him. Now come on."

She put her shoulder against Peony's, and together the three began to walk into the Northern Forest.

# CHAPTER SEVEN

LEAF STOOD UP ON her back paws, her front paws placed carefully on top of the rock, and peered over the top toward the entrance to the cave.

They'd almost walked right past it, journeying through a rocky and sparse part of the Northern Forest, following Pepper's directions as he tried to recall which way he'd seen Rain going. Then Dasher had jumped and butted his head against Leaf's leg, and they'd all seen the dark cave, and heard the scuffling of a creature behind the rustling curtain of dry vines that grew over the entrance.

It had seemed safest to hide while they decided what to do.

Leaf dropped back down behind the rock. "We have to go inside and check," she whispered. "What if it's Rain?"

"It probably is Rain," Pepper said. "I'm sure she came this way!"

"Oh, good idea," said Dasher slyly. "Why don't you go and look, since you're the one who saw her? Thanks for volunteering."

Pepper gave Leaf a startled look, and Leaf sighed.

"You said you'd be nice," she muttered to Dasher. "He's trying to help." She understood that the red panda didn't quite trust Pepper yet, and her brother was definitely *odd*, and maybe he had a tendency to exaggerate when he shouldn't. But they had no choice but to follow him. They had to find Rain!

"Well, I'm not sticking my nose in that cave on his say-so," Dasher sniffed.

"Well, *I'll* stick my nose under every rock in the Bamboo Kingdom if it means I find my sister," Leaf declared. She padded out of their hiding place and up toward the cave, her steps confident and strong, at least for the first bear-length or so. As she drew closer to the twitching vines, she slowed down, stepping carefully over the rocks.

"Hello?" she said quietly, still from a whole bear-length away.

There was no answer, but the vines went still.

Swallowing, Leaf stepped even closer, and peered inside, poking her nose just past the vines.

"Is someone there? Rain?"

She couldn't see anything in the deep shadows . . . and then a pair of eyes opened. They glinted bright and furious orange as they glared at Leaf. The shadows stirred, long fur rippling, jaws opening in a hiss of rage. The thing leaped at Leaf, and she yelped and threw herself backward, in such a hurry to get away that she tripped and rolled onto her back.

The creature burst from its cave and pounced onto Leaf, placing its fluffy front paws on her belly as if she were a mouse it had caught.

It was a manul cat. It was less than half Leaf's size, but she didn't dare move—its grumpy-looking face was close to hers, and its sharp predator's teeth were still bared.

"What do you want?" the cat snarled.

"Sorry! I didn't mean any offense!" Leaf squeaked.

The manul sniffed at Leaf, then hopped off her and sat by the entrance of her cave, cleaning her long, fluffy brown fur.

"Hmph. *More* pandas." She shook her head, her tongue still sticking out from grooming one paw. "Don't think I can't smell you over there, you two."

Leaf managed to sit up, and Pepper and Dasher slunk out from behind the rock.

"I'm sorry we disturbed you," Leaf said. "I'm Leaf, and this is my brother Pepper and my friend Dasher."

The manul regarded Leaf with a long, cold glare. "My name is my own," she said. "You may address me as Finest. And now you may leave me alone. Your friends are long gone."

"Our friends?" Leaf gasped. "Did you see another panda pass by here? Maybe one with a white grip pad, just like this?" She held up her paw. Finest stopped cleaning herself and sniffed at the grip pad suspiciously, then went back to grooming her long, fluffy chest fur.

"I didn't see them that closely," she said. "But yes, I saw

another panda. A big group of them, *and* red pandas."

*The Northern Forest pandas!* Leaf thought, exchanging an excited look with Dasher. *They must have left the Darkpool and moved on. Rain could be with them!*

"They came stomping through my territory and scaring all the prey," Finest went on. "So if you're sticking your nose in my cave looking for them, let me tell you, there isn't room for that clumsy crowd in there. They moved on, and so should you."

"We will," Leaf said, her heart swelling. "Where did they go?"

Finest rolled her eyes.

"That way," she said, pointing with one paw. Leaf turned to look and saw a ridge that sloped down, toward an area with more trees and greenery "Go on, scram."

"Thank you, Finest!" Leaf said, bowing deeply before the cat. This seemed to please Finest, at least a little. She stopped grooming herself and sat up very straight to watch Leaf, Pepper, and Dasher hurry away along the ridge.

"It's the Slenderwood pandas," Dasher said as he trotted alongside Leaf, picking their way over the rocks and down the long slope. "Or Darkpool, or whatever they're calling themselves now. And my family's still with them!"

"Why do we want to go to where these other pandas are?" Pepper asked. There was a sulky edge to his voice, and when Leaf looked around, she saw that he was lagging a bit behind, dragging his paws.

"They're our family!" she said. "And if Rain went this way,

she probably met up with them after all!"

"I can't wait to see my mother again," Dasher said. "And Jumper and Chomper, and Splasher and Wanderer and all the others."

"If Rain and Plum split up, maybe Plum's found them too," said Leaf. She longed to see her aunt again, the panda who had raised and guided her since she was just a tiny cub. They'd get all the triplets together, at last, and then Plum would know what to do next.

The ridge began to slope more and more steeply under their paws, until the journey became more of a climb than a walk.

"I don't think Rain came this way," Pepper said. Leaf looked up and saw him standing on a rock a few bear-lengths back, looking down as if the short clamber below him was a sheer cliff. "I think she would have gone another way. What if we're following this group and she isn't with them? Would the group have climbed down this way anyway?"

"It's all right," Leaf said soothingly. "It's not as scary as it looks."

"It's not that!" Pepper yelped, a bit too quickly. "What about Rain?"

"If she's not with the others, then we'll retrace our steps and find her trail," Leaf said. "I promise, it's okay. If the rock feels a bit high, then turn around and let yourself down back paws first—it's easier."

Pepper gave her a skeptical look, but he finally turned himself around and slid clumsily over the edge of the rock and down to the next part of the slope.

"That's it! Come on, I'll stay with you and show you some tricks. We're built for climbing and falling, us pandas. Big, soft, furry behinds to land on!"

That got a chuckle out of Pepper. Leaf glanced down toward the bottom of the slope and saw that Dasher was already scrambling several bear-lengths ahead. He looked up at Pepper and rolled his eyes, which Leaf thought was very unkind of him.

She helped Pepper to clamber down one ledge after another, and to Pepper's credit, he was keen to learn the tricks to finding the best paw holds and swinging his body as he fell so he wouldn't land with a bump on the sharp edge of a rock. It felt good to be climbing, even slowly.

Finally, the ground began to even out, the gaps between rocks grew shallower, and the paths between them could be walked on again, if Leaf placed her paws carefully and looked out for loose pebbles. She peered ahead, but the path ran under a wide evergreen branch, and she couldn't see beyond its spray of bright needles until she ducked underneath.

Suddenly, on the other side, the rocks under her paws gave way to earth and grass, and she found herself looking down a long, winding slope dotted with pine trees, toward a bright clearing with the distinctive long shapes of bamboo growing at its edge—and black-and-white and red creatures moving around it.

"It's them!" Dasher came bounding back up the slope

toward her. "We found them!"

"Come on, Pepper!" Leaf yelped, and started to trot down to the clearing.

"She might not be there," Pepper muttered, but he stayed with Leaf as they approached the other pandas.

Leaf looked around at the clearing as they entered through a gap in the trees. It seemed like a nice place to settle—she hoped that this time the pandas might have gotten lucky. At the very least there was obviously more bamboo here than there had been in the Slenderwood, and no poisoned pools that she could see. . . .

"Leaf!" a voice cried out, after she'd taken no more than a few steps into the clearing. "It's Leaf and Dasher! They found us!"

Within seconds, the clearing was filled with pandas and red pandas, dropping out of the trees, hurrying across the grass, calling out welcomes. It was a wonderful contrast to the listless sickness that had greeted them when they'd arrived at the Darkpool. Leaf was delighted to see Cane barreling toward her on strong little legs, any weakness from his brush with the poisoned water apparently forgotten. He couldn't seem to stop himself in time and he ran right into her, and she put a paw around him and licked him hard on the forehead.

"Dasher!"

Seeker Climbing Far, Dasher's mother, was right behind Cane, and she wriggled through the crowd to nuzzle her head against his.

"Dragon Speaker," said Gale, bowing to Leaf. "We're so glad you've found us again." Several of the other pandas dipped their heads too. Leaf smiled and nodded back. It was such a relief to be believed, especially when she was claiming something that sounded so wild but it still felt awkward to have pandas like Gale and Juniper bow to her and ask her opinion, when they'd known her all her life!

Leaf looked around at Pepper and motioned for him to come forward. She placed a paw on his shoulder and grinned at her family with pride.

"Everybody? I'd like you to meet someone. This is my brother, Pepper," she said. "My other triplet—he's a Dragon Speaker too!"

"H-hello," said Pepper shyly.

The pandas gasped.

"You found him!" said Grass. She bowed even lower. "Greetings, Dragon Speaker."

The others echoed her words—*Dragon Speaker, Speaker Pepper*—and soon every creature in the clearing was bowing, except for Dasher, and a couple of other red pandas at the back of the crowd who were jostling for a better view.

Leaf searched their faces while they were all still for a moment—but there was no sign of Rain or Plum. She sighed. She supposed it couldn't have been that easy to finally unite all three triplets.

Pepper looked stricken for a moment, his eyes darting across the faces of the pandas. Then he took a deep breath and drew himself up. He gave a solemn nod. "My pandas," he said, "thank you for your greetings. I can't wait to get to know all of you."

"It's time for the Feast of Long Light," said Crabapple. "You will join us, won't you?"

"Of course," said Pepper, before Leaf could speak. "We would be honored."

*He's taken to this pretty well,* Leaf thought, with a stifled chuckle, as her own stomach gave a happy rumble at the thought of a real feast, with enough bamboo to go around.

The pandas led them into the center of the clearing and then bustled off to fetch the bamboo. Dasher and his mother vanished up a tree, and soon the branches were full of red pandas holding fruits and nuts and insects and even some bamboo, ready to share the feast with their friends. It made Leaf's heart swell to see them all, still together even after all they'd been through.

"Pepper," said Hyacinth, holding out a bamboo cane to him, "will you do us the honor of saying the blessing?"

"Um . . . ," Pepper said. He looked at Leaf. "Yes, of course. But both of us Dragon Speakers should say it together, right?"

"Oh. All right," Leaf said with a smile. She met his eyes, waiting for him to begin. But it seemed like he was waiting for her. So she wriggled in the grass, picked up her own bamboo cane, and then began. "Great Dragon, at the Feast of Long Light your humble pandas bow before you. . . ."

She paused. It was odd—Pepper was speaking the words

too, but his were just a little behind hers, and when she stopped, he did too.

*Do you not know the blessings?* she wondered. Then she felt terrible for Pepper—of course he might not know them. He said he'd been separated from their mother for a long time, and then he was found by Sunset and the monkeys. He might never have known the comfort that was a family of pandas who always feasted together, hearing the Dragon's blessing over and over until they could recite the virtues in their sleep.

She finished the blessing, thanking the Dragon for the bamboo and the endurance it bestowed on them.

The sound of crunching as every panda bit into their bamboo was beautiful to Leaf's ears. She took a deep sniff of her own cane and started to pick the leaves off, using her grip pad to make a big, juicy bunch of them. She glanced at Pepper, just to check he was all right, and saw him holding his bamboo cane and staring, narrow-eyed, across at the one that Grass was holding.

"What's the matter?" she asked.

Pepper looked at her thoughtfully. "Is this really right?" he asked. "I mean, we're Dragon Speakers. Should we really eat the same food as everyone else? The Dragon Speaker's the most important panda in the whole kingdom, right? So we should get the best food! You, there," he called, before Leaf could stop him. "I want to swap bamboo with you."

Grass looked up, halfway through chewing on a mouthful of leaves.

"Wha—?"

"You've got more leaves on yours," Pepper explained, as if it were the most obvious thing in the world. "Swap with me."

Hesitantly, Grass held her cane out toward Pepper. He snatched it from her and threw his own down, just barely in reach, so she had to lean all the way over to get it.

Leaf stared at him in shock. She glanced around and saw that several of the other pandas were staring at Pepper too— and some of them were staring at *her*, bewildered looks on their faces. She started to feel hot with embarrassment. Up in the branches of a nearby tree, she spotted Dasher, who had dropped one of his fruits in astonishment and was making an exaggeratedly scandalized face. *What does he think he's doing?*

"Pepper," Leaf said, trying to keep her voice gentle. "I don't think that's how Dragon Speakers are supposed to behave."

"Oh?" Pepper said, through a mouthful of bamboo bark. "Oh, I see. Thank you, faithful panda," he said to Grass with a patronizing little bow.

Crabapple, specifically, was looking at Leaf with a piercing glare that clearly said, *You might be the Dragon Speaker, but I'll still give you a piece of my mind if you make me . . .*

Leaf opened her mouth to scold Pepper once more, and then stopped.

Another panda had appeared at the edge of the clearing— one she didn't know. It was a large, adult female. She didn't walk as if she belonged with the other pandas, but came forward gingerly, several bamboo canes held in her jaws. One by one, the other pandas noticed her. She put down the canes and spoke.

"Excuse me for interrupting your feast," she said.

At the sound of her voice, Pepper looked up, and the bamboo slipped out of his paws and onto the ground with a rustle.

"I wondered if I might . . . ," the panda began, looking around at the assembled bears. Then her eyes lit on Pepper, and she gasped. "Pepper? Oh, Pepper, is it really you?"

"Um. Uh. It—I—" Pepper stammered.

"Who are you?" Leaf asked, although she felt a tingle start at the back of her neck, like she already knew the answer.

"I'm his mother," said the panda.

". . . Orchid?" Leaf whispered.

"What? No," the panda said, and Leaf's tingles seemed to turn into sharp pine needles against her skin. "My name's Goji. Pepper, what have you been telling these pandas? I've been looking for you for a whole moon!"

"Wait. . . ." Leaf could barely hear the panda speak over the pounding of her own heart. "A moon? Not any longer?"

"Leaf?" Crabapple said. "What's going on? This isn't Orchid—why is she saying she's Pepper's mother?"

Leaf looked at Pepper. He met her eyes and then looked away, apparently lost for words, more or less for the first time.

A chilly calm came over her all of a sudden. It all made sense: Pepper's strange way of following Rain's trail, the way the monkeys had reacted to him, and even—Leaf felt a little sick—the bitten-off grip pad.

"I'm so sorry, everyone," she said, getting to her paws. "I've made a terrible mistake. Pepper's not a Dragon Speaker at all. He's not my triplet—he's a liar!"

# CHAPTER EIGHT

"HURRY UP, SLOWBELLY," SAID Jitterpaws, rapping her knuckles against a tree trunk.

Ghost sighed and kept walking at his own pace, his stomach clenching and twisting with every step.

He was pretty sure they were getting close to the Broken Forest, and he was still not sure what he was going to do. He wanted to just leave the three monkeys and slip away, but it was almost as if *they* were bringing *him* somewhere, not the other way around. Whether they were climbing rocky slopes or crossing streams or traveling along the sides of forest valleys, Jitterpaws, Sweetfur, and Heavyfist had stuck to walking alongside him instead of leaping up into the branches of trees.

*Do they know?* he wondered. *What if they suspect that Sunset's lied to them about the squirrels, and they're waiting to beat the truth out of me?*

*Well, then I'll tell them the truth,* he thought. *That's easy. I just want to do it quickly.*

The sun was going down, casting thin red shafts of light between the trunks of the trees as they climbed a hill between tall, twisted pines. At this rate, they wouldn't even reach the Broken Forest before it was dark, and he *certainly* wouldn't make it back to the Southern Forest and the river path before Moon Climb.

He told himself there was still time: If he could find a way to turn back soon, if Nimbletail waited just a little longer before starting her run to lure the guards away, if Rain and Peony took a while to climb out of the pit . . . he could still be there.

He tried not to let himself think about what would happen if they were caught and he hadn't made it back.

Suddenly the trees ended, and Ghost found himself looking at a desolate hillside that seemed to blaze with burning spots of light. As the monkeys urged him onward, he realized that the scrubby ground was dotted with small bushes with deep red leaves and red starburst flowers. They reflected the setting sun and made the whole hillside look like it was on fire.

On the other side of the bushes, the hillside crested and then fell away, and Ghost looked down at the strangest place he had ever seen.

The Broken Forest wasn't just a dramatic name. On the other side of the hill, a huge valley sat in deep shadow. It was so big and so dark that it gave Ghost the strange feeling that the sun could never climb high enough to reach the darkness at the center. All the way down the slope from the ridge where he stood, as far as Ghost could see, scattered and splintered tree branches and bamboo canes littered the ground. Stumps stuck out like jagged teeth, some with fragile new growth, moss and fungus climbing up their sides, others black and dead. Even the rocks were broken and scattered across the bare earth.

"What *is* this place?" Ghost had to force himself to step over the crest of the hill, to pad down to the first row of broken tree stumps. "I had no idea . . . the Broken Forest . . ." He turned and looked back at the three monkeys. "*This* is your new territory? Why would you want this place?"

Sweetfur grinned at him, and Jitterpaws tapped excitedly on the ground in front of her.

Ghost felt his fur begin to prickle, starting at the tips of his paws and creeping up his back, over his neck. Why were they looking at him like that?

"Look again," said Heavyfist.

He didn't want to look. But he had to. He turned back around.

The monkeys emerged from behind the rocks, from inside the hollow stumps, almost as if they were stepping from thin air. Dozens of them. The whole Southern Forest troop must be here. No . . . there were *more* of them than that, more than Ghost had ever seen before, swarming out of the shadows of the Broken Forest.

He tried to take a step back, but felt something push against his flank, and spun around to see Jitterpaws and Heavyfist right against him, flanked by another five or ten monkeys who seemed to have come out of nowhere.

He was completely surrounded.

He started to try to growl, to warn these monkeys that he wouldn't be intimidated, even though the fear in his veins was making his white fur stand on end. He had to stop turning on the spot, but he was afraid that if he did, then the monkeys behind him would close in even more. . . .

One of the monkeys stepped forward, out of the broken tree line. It was Brawnshanks. Ghost focused on his flat blue face as he walked toward him. His skin felt hot under his fur.

"You tricked Sunset," he muttered. "Your monkeys wanted me to come here, didn't they? Why? Just so I could see it?" He cast another nervous glance at the broken trees and the horde of monkeys hanging from every splintered branch.

"Oh no," said Brawnshanks. "I didn't trick Sunset—not on this occasion, anyway."

The monkeys behind him laughed. It was a horrible, high, rattling sound. From where Ghost was standing, the echoes seemed to fill the dark valley behind them.

"No, I told him the truth. You see, my spies found the panda cub called Pepper, alive and well in the Northern Forest. Now, what do you think Sunset felt when I told him you'd lied to him about killing the cub?"

The anxious heat fell away, and Ghost felt cold all over, as if he'd just been plunged into deep snow.

"He wants you dead," Brawnshanks said. "He sent you up here to die. Now, I don't much care what that old faker wants—"

"I won't do it," Ghost burst out. "I don't care what you want. I'm sick of doing everyone's dirty work."

"Noble sentiment." Brawnshanks sneered. "But unfortunately for you, what I want happens to align with Sunset, for now. *I want you dead too.*"

Ghost flinched, and tried to back away, but Brawnshanks moved like lightning and grabbed onto his ear, bringing his face close so that only Ghost would hear him.

"You see, I worked it out," he hissed. "I know who you are. Who you *really* are."

"What?" Ghost gasped, as Brawnshanks pulled back. "Wait, what do you mean?"

But Brawnshanks's only reply was a flail of his arm as he walked away, and then the other monkeys were starting to advance, their lips peeling back in horrible grins that showed their sharp, jagged teeth.

For a moment, Ghost was too frightened to do anything but watch them close in.

Then he shook himself hard, imagining himself bursting from the thick blanket of snow that had settled over him, the fur standing up all along his back. He crouched low and roared, and raked his claws on the ground.

"Come on, then!" he growled.

*Whatever Brawnshanks thinks he knows, I'm a cub Born of Winter, and we don't go down without a fight!*

"Come on!" he yelled again. "You might kill me, but I'll take down a hundred of you before I go! Who wants to be first?"

The monkeys hopped and jittered just out of range of his claws.

Then a whoop sounded behind him, and he felt a heavy weight thump down on his back. Long fingers grabbed onto his ears, and teeth scraped the skin on his neck.

Ghost threw himself down and rolled over, and there was a satisfying squeak of surprise and pain from the monkey who'd jumped on him.

But now the other monkeys were piling in with grabbing fingers and biting jaws. Ghost managed to get back to his paws, leaving the monkey he'd thrown off—Heavyfist, he realized—groaning on the ground, and then he lashed out, claws scything through the air and catching fur and flesh. All he could see now in the fading light was a swarm of monkey limbs and snarling faces. He felt little bursts of pain as their claws and teeth dug into him, and paid each one back with a stomp of claws or a snap of teeth that sent the monkeys flying, blood spattering across the broken ground.

*I was raised a predator!* Ghost thought desperately, as wave after wave of monkeys piled onto him. *Winter, be with me . . . if I'm going to die, help me make them hurt for it. . . .*

One of the monkeys got its long fingers into his ear and

snapped at his face, sharp teeth grazing close to Ghost's right eye, and he roared and tore the monkey off with a swipe of his claws. He felt the body under his paw twitch and go still.

There was blood in his teeth and soaked into the fur on his paws, and still the monkeys came, howling with fury and mad laughter. His right eye was closing all on its own, narrowing his vision. He lashed out to the right and his paw found nothing there, and all the monkeys cackled. He felt blood trickling through his fur, bites and scratches knitting together like a stinging spiderweb. He tried to use the pain to keep his anger burning.

But he was getting tired. And for every monkey that lay dead or bleeding near him, it seemed there were a hundred more, fresh and eager, just waiting for their chance. He screamed and lunged at the closest one, but he was too slow. His teeth snapped on empty air and he felt the monkey's paws scratch over his nose.

One of them slipped between his paws, and Ghost flailed, trying to catch it, and staggered, and almost fell. The monkeys whooped and laughed again—

And then their chuckles changed to worried chatter.

"No! Not you!" Ghost heard Brawnshanks shrieking. He looked up through his one good eye and saw the golden-monkey leader astride a tall splintered tree trunk nearby, pointing up to the crest of the hill. "Bring him down!"

A roar echoed through the valley, loud and strange.

*Winter . . . ?* Ghost thought. But the monkeys had heard it too. They hesitated in their attacks. Several of them peeled away from him. He looked around.

A tiger stalked down the slope, his orange tail lashing and bright eyes fixed on the monkeys that charged toward him, the muscles rippling below his flanks. Ghost froze. The tiger's huge jaws were open and snarling.

"Run!" the tiger roared at Ghost.

One of the monkeys leaped, and the tiger lunged forward and snatched it right out of the air and tossed it away, limbs flailing, to strike a bamboo stump and lie still. Ghost flinched as if he'd felt the jaws close around his own flesh. "Ghost! Run!" the tiger commanded again.

*He knows me,* Ghost thought, bewildered. He turned, forcing his exhausted, stinging limbs into movement. He barreled directly at the monkeys who'd been behind him, hurling one aside and trampling the other.

"No!" he heard Brawnshanks scream behind him. "Stop that bear!"

But the monkeys were confused and afraid. One lashed out as he passed it and managed to grab on to his fur, but he just kept running, brushing against a jagged rock. The rock caught the monkey face-first; its grip failed, and it tumbled back down the slope.

Ghost ran on, the muscles in his legs and the tears on his paw pads screaming with pain as he climbed to the top of the hill. The distance that had seemed like nothing on the way down felt like climbing the White Spine Mountains now, but at last he staggered over the lip of the valley and dived into the shadow of one of the red bushes. The sun was gone, and the dark red leaves looked like drying blood as he peered over the crest of the hill and back down toward the Broken Forest.

The tiger was nothing but a few flashes of orange and black under a sea of biting, scratching monkeys. Brawnshanks was still screaming. The tiger writhed and roared.

Ghost knew he should leave, that the fact that no monkey seemed to have seen where he'd gone was a blessing from the Snow Cat that he couldn't count on for long.

But the tiger had saved his life. And there was nothing he could do to return the favor. He knew it in his aching bones. He was too tired, had lost too much, to stop the relentless pounding of the monkeys. He could only watch in horror as the tiger's roars turned to pained cries, and then to silence as he stopped fighting back.

"Enough," Brawnshanks commanded at last. He stormed into the group of monkeys and tore them from the tiger's flank, almost as violent with his own kind as they'd been with Ghost. He looked down at the tiger's closed eyes and screamed right in his face, a shriek of rage that made Ghost's blood run cold. Then he turned away.

"Find me that panda," Ghost heard him snarl to one of the other monkeys, grabbing it by the throat as he passed by. "Come back with news that he's dead, or *never* come back." He released the monkey, and it ran away, up the hill, straight past Ghost's hiding place, gibbering with fright.

The rest of the monkeys began to vanish back into the forest, the maze of broken branches swallowing them one by one. Those who couldn't walk were dragged, and others limped, clutching claw wounds. Several didn't move at all, and wouldn't ever again.

Ghost waited, holding his breath, until he was as certain as he could be that they weren't waiting for him just out of sight.

Then he pushed his way out of the bush and stumbled, as fast as he could, down the slope toward the tiger.

He was crumpled on the rocky earth, huge paws limp and eyes closed. For a horrible moment, Ghost could see once more the shape of Winter, lying unmoving at the bottom of the Endless Maw.

Ghost lay down, his chin resting on his own bleeding paws, beside the tiger.

"Why?" he whispered. "Why did you do this?"

The tiger stirred. One eye peeled open, weeping and sore, and looked up at him.

"You're alive!" Ghost gasped, and leaped to his paws. "What can I do? Can you get up? If you can lean on me, then . . ."

"Shhh." The tiger turned his head toward him, but the effort seemed to exhaust him, and his flanks heaved as he gasped for breath. "Listen to me, Ghost."

His words were so faint, Ghost had to lie back down on his belly, putting his ear close to the tiger's mouth, to hear them clearly. Just moments ago, Ghost would have been terrified to be this close to the huge predator, a creature that had frightened Sunset so much he refused to cross the river. But now he felt safer beside the tiger, even though he was mortally wounded, than he had in a long time.

"Go to the White Spine," the tiger rasped. Ghost caught his breath. "Find the panda's jaws and . . . the tiger's eye . . . the ancient rocks . . . the Dragon Speaker . . . and the Watcher." He paused, wincing, a huge shiver rippling through his striped fur. "Between them. There is a tunnel. Inside, a . . . a blue stone. Take it. Save us all. Save . . . the kingdom. . . ."

"A blue stone?" Ghost whispered. "Like Sunset has? You mean it really does something? But where are these ancient rocks? What does any of this mean?"

But the tiger didn't answer. His breath stilled, and his eye drooped closed once more.

Sadness washed over Ghost, a horrible echo of the pain of Winter's death that had swept him away from the White Spine Mountains. He staggered to his paws and let out a long, exhausted sigh.

"I'm so sorry," he said. "I don't know how you know me, or why you did this! But I'll . . . I'll do as you ask. If it can stop Sunset and Brawnshanks, I'll go back to the mountains and look for the stone."

He put his muzzle to the fur between the tiger's eyes and gave it a small, sad lick before turning and limping up out of the Broken Forest valley once more.

# CHAPTER NINE

LEAF STARED AT PEPPER. He couldn't meet her eyes, and she didn't blame him.

*Why?*

That was the question that the Northern Forest pandas had been trying unsuccessfully to solve all afternoon. The initial uproar had taken some time to die away: Pepper had tried to double down, insisting that he was a Dragon Speaker, that he had special powers! But the truth was not in doubt, not with Goji there to contradict almost everything he'd said about his life so far. Pepper's mother had been equal parts apologetic and defensive; the other adult pandas had been angry; the red pandas had come down from the trees to listen and speculate and try to question Pepper. Even now, as the Feast of Sun Fall was approaching, nothing felt at all resolved.

"I still can't believe you hurt yourself for this," Goji sighed, nuzzling Pepper's head. Pepper sat stiffly and looked at the ground. "Biting off your own grip pad, all so they would think it had been white, and you were one of them!"

"He must have had a reason," said Crabapple darkly. "What if he was sent by Sunset to lure Leaf off the path? He must be a traitor!"

"No!" Goji gasped. "He's no traitor, he's just . . . he's always made up stories, ever since he was a tiny cub. He just wants to be at the center of everything, and since we got separated . . . maybe you were desperate for somewhere to belong. Right, Pepper?"

"That's no reason to lie about something this important," growled Wanderer Leaping High. "There *is* no good reason for it."

"Pepper, what were you trying to achieve?" Leaf asked, not for the first time. "Is it true—did you just want to feel important?"

Pepper spoke in a small voice. "I heard pandas talking. About the triplets, and how important they were, and I just . . ." He pawed the ground. "They said I was one—I never told them I was! And I could have been! *You* had siblings you'd never even met, right?" He looked at Leaf. "You didn't know I *wasn't* your brother, so . . . so maybe I could be! Only, the Dragon Speaker didn't like me; he wanted me dead! So he sent a white panda to kill me, and I ran away, until I found you. . . ."

Leaf shook her head as she listened to this garbled story.

"How can we believe anything you say?" she said.

She could see Dasher out of the corner of her eye, look-ing furious. Even though he hadn't been completely fooled, he seemed to be taking this as hard as any of the others. She couldn't bring herself to look directly at him. She had taken Pepper's side all the way here, through the mud and the boars and the monkeys. . . .

"It doesn't matter why he did it," said Wanderer again. "The question is, what do we do with him now?"

"*Do* with him?" asked Hyacinth nervously.

"Whether he's a spy for Sunset Deepwood, or just inca-pable of telling the truth, I don't think we want him as a Hollowtree," Crabapple said. "I say we kick them out, both of them."

"Where will we go?" Pepper asked.

"Anywhere, as long as it's far from here and we never have to see you again," Crabapple growled.

Goji put a protective paw on Pepper's shoulder again. "We'll be all right," she said. But Leaf could hear the doubt in her voice. She remembered that Goji had only come upon the group because she'd been looking for somewhere to stay, someone to share her bamboo with. Was she lonely, after she'd lost her cub? Had she been searching for something to eat for a long time?

"Yeah," said another of the red pandas. "We don't need this weird cub making our lives difficult."

Juniper chimed in to agree, and then more of the Leaping

Highs and the Digging Deeps. The clearing rang with the voices of pandas agreeing that they would be better off throwing Pepper out, and Goji with him.

"No," Leaf said loudly.

The others fell silent and looked at her. She looked back evenly, trying not to seem nervous as she waited for their attention. She saw, in Crabapple's and Wanderer's eyes, the moment that they remembered that a true Dragon Speaker was among them. Wanderer had been standing up on his back legs, and he sank back down on all fours and dipped his head in recognition.

*Oh, Dragon, now they're all expecting me to say something wise! Please, help me. . . .*

She paused, just on the faint chance that the Dragon might actually send her a sign—but there was no shadow among the trees, no meaningful stirring of the air.

Leaf sat up as tall as she could. She thought for a moment, looking at Pepper, and then at the rest of the group.

*This is part of being a Dragon Speaker. Not just visions and destiny. I have to trust my instincts, and if I get it wrong . . . then I'll make it right.*

"Pepper shouldn't have lied," she said. "But I don't think he even really knows why he was doing it. I don't think he can help it. And I don't think we can punish him for something he can't help. We need to be merciful. We should let him and Goji stay with us."

She was half expecting Crabapple or Wanderer or one of the others to argue with her—but nobody did. There were a few sighs, as if the pandas were resigning themselves to a path that annoyed them, but not a single voice was raised in dissent.

Leaf struggled not to show how frightening that was.

*They all just . . . agreed with what I said, because I said it.*

Goji bowed low, pressing her chin to the grass at Leaf's feet, and then sat up and held Pepper close. "Thank you, Dragon Speaker. I promise, Pepper meant no harm, and we will be no trouble."

Leaf stepped forward and touched her nose to Goji's, and then Pepper's.

"Welcome," she said. And then, just as she'd hoped, some of the pandas and the red pandas—not Crabapple, but Hyacinth and Cane, and Seeker and some others—came forward to welcome them too.

Leaf backed away, relieved to have passed the focus of the crowd on to someone else.

No wonder a bad panda like Sunset would want anyone to think he was the Dragon Speaker. It wasn't about getting the best bamboo, though she was sure he probably did—it was a much deeper, more dangerous kind of power. . . .

Leaf stretched out along the tree branch, her back paws resting comfortably in a hollow against the trunk. She was pleased with it as a sleeping place—she could look down into the clearing and see the pandas who were sleeping on the ground curling up in their places: Goji and Pepper together in a tight circle of black and white, near Hyacinth and Cane, and a wriggling pile of red and striped fur that looked to be all the Digging Deeps, cuddled together in a nest they'd made for themselves in a pile of fallen gingko leaves.

"Hi," said a small voice. "Can I join you?"

She looked up to see Dasher walking along the next branch over.

"Yes, please," she said. Dasher hopped across to her branch, and settled down with his head beside hers. He closed his eyes. "I'm so sorry, Dasher," she whispered. "I'm sorry I didn't believe you about Pepper. I'm sorry I let him walk us halfway across the kingdom for no reason!"

"I get it," said Dasher, opening his eyes and turning his head to look at her. "I could see how badly you wanted him to be real. And I never guessed *how* wrong he was."

Leaf gave him a weak smile. "You didn't say I *told you so*. You can, if you want."

"Nah," said Dasher. "The truth is, I wish I'd been wrong. We're back down to one triplet out of three. We've still got to find Rain, as well as the other one, whoever they are, wherever they are."

"We'll find a way," said Leaf, with more certainty than she felt.

Dasher put his small paws over her big one. "We will," he said.

He closed his eyes again and tucked his paws under himself, and it wasn't long before Leaf could tell from his soft, even breaths that he was fast asleep.

She wished she could be too. But even though she ached from all the walking, and the clearing was peaceful, she just couldn't seem to find her way to sleep.

*What am I going to do?* she thought. *Rain probably never came this way—and whether she did or not, it's no use asking Pepper.*

*And Pepper . . . why did we even meet him? If all he did was lie to us, why would the Dragon send the bats to lead me to that cave? Was it all just a terrible mistake? Was Rain actually nearby, and we just missed her? If only we'd been there earlier, if only we'd waited longer. . . .*

But there was no use wishing that sort of thing now. The Dragon had sent the bats, and the bats had taken her down this path, whether they meant to or not. Now what she needed was just a little bit of help to find the way back. . . .

She lay there, not sleeping, as the stars shone overhead and the tiny, almost-invisible sliver of the moon moved across the sky. When it was finally time for the Feast of Moon Fall, she was one of the first to get up. She slid down the trunk of the tree, trying not to wake Dasher or the other Climbing Fars who had taken up positions in the same network of branches.

The pandas gathered quietly. They always did, for this nighttime feast, the ninth and last. Leaf was pleased to see that Cane was old enough to join them now—he used to sleep through it, when they were Slenderwoods, saving his energy for the new day, but now he was bright-eyed and obviously hungry. Goji and Pepper joined them too, and they formed a small circle in the middle of the clearing, surrounded by the soft sounds of snoring red pandas.

"Great Dragon, at the Feast of Moon Fall your humble pandas bow before you. Thank you for the gift of the bamboo, and the unity you bestow upon us."

It felt good to speak those words at the first official feast of Goji's and Pepper's life with the Northern Forest pandas.

Normally, Moon Fall was a quiet feast and the pandas would go straight back to sleep after they'd eaten, but Leaf approached Gale as she was making her way back to the tree she'd made her nest in.

"Gale, can I ask you something?"

"Of course, Dragon Speaker. Leaf," Gale added, more softly. "What is it?"

"Earlier, Crabapple called this place Hollowtree, right? Why is that?"

"Oh, we're close to the Hollow Fir!" Gale said, excitement breaking through her sleepiness. "It's one of the sacred places in the Northern Forest. Before the flood, it was one of the places the Dragon Speaker would go to send his word to pandas across the kingdom."

"Wow," Leaf murmured. Of course, she'd heard that Dragon Speakers had done this in the past—that the way they'd helped creatures all over the kingdom was by passing their visions on to the other pandas, making them their emissaries to the other animals. It had always been a fun story, something to imagine while she sat at the top of the Grandfather Gingko in the Slenderwood and stared out over the river.

*But if it's true, and I'm the Dragon Speaker now . . . should I be able to do that?*

She had no idea how she would begin to do such a thing. But another idea was starting to form in her mind. If this Hollow Fir was a sacred place, where the Dragon's power could be felt . . .

"It's that way," said Gale, giving her a small, knowing smile and pointing with her muzzle into the trees. "You can't miss it."

"Thank you!" Leaf said.

She didn't even try to go back to the tree and get some sleep. She was wide awake, and now her heart was starting to stir with hope again.

Gale was right—she couldn't miss the Hollow Fir. She only had to weave between the trees for a short distance before something large loomed in front of her, a tree with a patch of deeper darkness at its heart. She sniffed her way up to it, fascinated, and discovered that something had made the tree form a sort of natural cave, with an entrance big enough for a panda. She went in carefully, thinking of Finest the manul cat, but there was nothing living inside except a beetle with shiny green wings that flashed at her as she passed.

Inside the tree, a thick and spongy carpet of moss had grown across the ground and up the walls. As the creeping brightness of Gray Light began to grow outside, Leaf could see that the moss covered the whole hollow, all the way to where the trunk came back together over her head. And there were tiny flowers growing in it, purple and white, scattered above like the stars in the sky.

Leaf looked up at them and tried to be as still as possible. She felt like she was waiting to feel the Dragon's presence, almost as if she was listening for a sound. But she heard nothing but the faint calls of birds, waking up in time for the dawn.

*Great Dragon . . . I'm still not sure how all this is supposed to work,* she thought. *I need you. You sent your bats to me, to show me it wasn't time to go to the mountain. They led me to Pepper, and Pepper led me here. But now I don't know what to do. I need to find my siblings. If you could send the bats again . . .*

She paused, taking a deep breath and closing her eyes. Perhaps she was asking too much, being too specific.

*Show me your will,* she thought, *and I'll do the best I can.*

When she opened her eyes again, the hollow seemed brighter than before. It was probably just the coming dawn, she thought—or perhaps she'd fallen asleep. But now she could make out the different shades of blue and purple in among the green moss, and see more of the shiny beetles making their way up and down the tree trunk.

But nothing else happened. She listened for the squeaking language of the bats, but they didn't seem to have come. The only thing she could hear was the growing chorus of birds outside. There was no sinuous shadow wrapped around her. No warm Dragon breath.

She sagged.

Perhaps the Dragon had its own plans, and it would show her in its own time.

Still, she couldn't help feeling impatient as she ducked back out of the Hollow Fir. She *had* to find Rain and their other triplet, and soon. . . .

She looked up at the sky and saw it was going to be another bright day—the ground was wreathed in mist, but the sky was a pure, pale color that told her the Feast of Gray Light was due.

Then a small black shape darted across the pale sky, and Leaf caught her breath. *Could it be?*

The shape landed in the branches of the tree and hung upside down from a twig, beating its leathery wings. It spoke, in its tiny little voice. Leaf's heart skipped a beat. She thought it had said, "Speaker!"

Another rustle of wings, and another bat landed in the tree, and then another, and then . . .

Leaf fell back onto her haunches, startled, as a crane with a red marking on its head in the shape of a gingko leaf landed right beside the bats, and then a second crane, which perched side by side with the first.

"You're not bats!" she exclaimed.

And they weren't the only ones. A bright, colorful blur rushed past her: a crowd of pheasants with their red chests, golden crowns, and striped blue backs. Doves, nightjars, kingfishers, and bee-eaters, and even a black eagle, whose arrival made every other bird and bat startle and scatter to other parts of the tree.

"Hello," said another small voice, and Leaf looked around

and saw a small gathering of flying squirrels, four of them, all sitting in a neat row along one branch. She found herself laughing at the sight of them, at the absurd mixture of creatures all sitting together, as well as for the sheer joy of knowing the Dragon had heard her.

*The Dragon has sent me every flying creature in the kingdom—or at least the ones who were close by!*

"What's up, Your Speakerness?" asked one of the squirrels. "We're here to help."

"We're not sure why," said another.

"We just got a . . . a big feeling," said the first. "Does that make sense?"

"Yes," said Leaf. She suddenly felt so overwhelmed with joy, she almost couldn't speak. "The Dragon sent you to help me."

There was a general cheeping and fluttering of wings at this. Leaf caught her breath.

"You can all understand me," she murmured. "Even the birds who I can't understand in return. . . . That's . . ." She cleared her throat. "Thank you for coming," she said. "I need your help. I'm looking for two other pandas—my triplets. They'd be cubs my age, with white grip pads, just like mine." She held up her paw. "One of them is called Rain. I don't know the other."

On the branch near the bats, the two cranes turned their long necks to look at each other, and took off at once. Leaf hoped with all her heart that that was a good sign. . . .

"Please, find my siblings and bring them to me, or take me

to them. Guide them and keep them from harm, if you can."

With a great rustle of wings, the branches of the Hollow Fir shook as every bird and bat and squirrel took off at once. Leaf watched as they rose into the sky, flapping, gliding, or spinning on the air, taking her hopes with them as they soared over the trees and disappeared.

# CHAPTER TEN

"THIS IS A TERRIBLE plan," said Shiver.

*I know,* Rain thought, peering through the thick clump of ferns. *It's by far the worst plan I've ever had. It might be the worst plan in the history of the Bamboo Kingdom.*

"It's the only plan I've got," she said out loud. "We can't just hide and regroup and take our time. Ghost's gone, who knows where—maybe he's dead, or turned to Sunset's side for real."

"He's not turned or dead," Shiver mewled.

"I don't know where Leaf ended up; she could be dead too for all I know," Rain went on. "We need to get rid of Sunset, for good, *now.*"

"I agree," said Peony. "We need to do this."

Rain looked down at her mother and wondered if Shiver was right after all. Peony was still very, very weak. The escape had taken almost all her strength, and even though they had managed to find her a few fruits to eat, and some clear water to drink, they hadn't been able to actually rest. The Feast of Gray Light had passed, and Sun Climb was well on its way. Rain couldn't remember the last time she'd had a full, satisfying meal.

"I think we might have lost them," Shiver said. She sounded relieved, but the words made Rain's chest clench with anxiety. "Maybe we should just go."

"We have to let them catch up," Rain muttered. "If they give up—or worse, if Sunset gives up and just sends Blossom after us—we'll never be able to lead him to the black pool the Dragon showed me. I'm supposed to get him there, I know it."

"How can we lead him there? You don't even know where it is!" Shiver hissed.

Rain wasn't sure what to say. She knew it sounded like foolishness, but she was certain it was *right*, too.

*Oh, Dragon—this must be how Leaf felt about the bats,* she thought suddenly. *I was so sure she was imagining things, and here I am doing exactly the same.*

Something moved on the other side of the ferns.

"Shh!" Rain said. She tried to focus. It could've been the wind, or some other animal passing through. They were still close to the river, where the undergrowth was thick. . . .

". . . need them back," came a growling voice, and a moment later Rain caught a glimpse of two—no, three—large pandas shouldering their way through the bushes between the trees.

Sunset, Ginseng, and Blossom were all still on their trail. Sunset was muttering angrily, and Rain got the impression he hadn't stopped in some time—the look on Blossom's face was even more thunderously grumpy than usual.

"Before they can poison the others against me," Sunset went on. "Disrespect to the Dragon Speaker is disrespect to the Great Dragon itself!"

*Who's he trying to fool?* Rain wondered. *They must know he's a fraud. . . . Maybe he's just trying to convince himself.*

"They were here—I can smell them," growled Blossom.

Rain tensed, ready to run.

"I—I don't smell anything," said another voice, and Rain's heart skipped a beat.

It was Pebble.

Rain saw Peony looking at her with deep sadness in her eyes, and looked away quickly. So what if Pebble was with them? Didn't Rain already know he'd chosen Sunset's side?

Actually knowing Pebble was with him still hurt, though, like a splinter in her paw.

"Rain! We have to go," Shiver hissed.

"Right," Rain said. "Ready?"

They burst from the ferns as one, and Rain heard Ginseng yell, "There they are!"

But the three of them were already on the move, and they had at least gotten some practice at this now. Shiver pulled ahead, her superior speed and grace meaning she could find the easiest route through the bushes. Peony went next, focusing on Shiver's white tail, following where she led. Rain brought up the rear, to make sure Peony wasn't left behind, listening all the time for their pursuers. They had to keep Sunset close, but if they were caught, she wasn't sure they could escape a second time. . . .

The shouting and crashing followed them through the trees, under splintered logs, and over piles of mossy rocks. The forest was growing denser: tall gingko and cypress trees with drooping branches that brushed the tops of the tallest bushes. Shiver had to wriggle and double back to find a way through. Rain hoped that Sunset was having even more trouble. . . .

Suddenly, Peony slowed. Rain skidded to a stop, almost running into her.

"Mother, are you all right?" she gasped.

"I'm fine," Peony panted. "Look!"

Ahead, between the trees, Shiver was standing exposed at the base of a tall cliff dripping with moss. She stared up at it, pacing back and forth, her tail swishing.

"I could make it to the top," she declared.

"But we can't." Rain looked over her shoulder. She couldn't see their pursuers, but she could hear them coming closer all the time.

"The trees, then," Peony suggested.

Rain looked up. Sure enough, the lowest branches of the trees were low enough for a panda to get to, and the higher ones looked sturdy enough to take them.

"We hide up there," Shiver agreed. "Till it's safe to go another way."

"Go," Rain said, and Shiver leaped, her long limbs stretching out to pull her up onto a branch with ease. Rain sighed. Not for the first time since she'd met Shiver, she wished she had a leopard's ability to jump. "You first," she told Peony, and sat at the base of the tree, holding out her paws. Peony focused her gaze on the branch and threw herself at the trunk, clambering up over Rain. Her paws slipped on a patch of moss and she almost fell back, but Rain kept the pressure on her back paws as she stood up to shove her mother upward. Her own tired back legs shook, but finally Peony found purchase on the bark and dragged herself up to the branch. Shiver was there, already showing Peony which branches were safe to climb to, leading her farther up and away from the cliffside, into the canopy of leaves.

Sunset was almost on them again now—Rain could hear him shouting at his thugs, telling them to clear a path. Would he be able to scent that they'd climbed the tree?

It was too late to change her mind. She leaped as high as she could up the tree and dug her claws in with all her might. She focused on what she'd learned from Shiver, and from Leaf, about looking for the best paw holds, and her back paws found a knot she could use to push against, and then a scratched place where some panda or other creature had sharpened their claws on the tree once and left a ridged place, perfect for getting a good grip. She avoided the damp moss and made it to the branch, then through the leaves and up higher, just in time. Black-and-white shapes barged into view below, and she pressed herself down in the crook of a branch, against the trunk of the tree, and tried to be completely still.

"Where did they go?" Sunset roared.

Rain peered down and saw Blossom and Ginseng scenting the ground. "They were here," Ginseng said.

"That's not what I asked you," Sunset said, lowering his voice dangerously and bringing his muzzle close to Ginseng's. "Find them!"

Pebble staggered into view too, and looked around just like the other two. Rain felt that splinter-like pain again, right in her heart.

"They couldn't have climbed this," Blossom said, staring up at the cliff. "Not with old Peony in the state she's in. They must have found a way around."

Sunset gave a great huff of annoyance and sat down. "Go and look," he told her. "Take the cub. Come back to me when you know which way they went."

He settled down with his back against one of the trees— not, to Rain's intense relief, the one she was in—and reached out to pluck a bamboo cane from the undergrowth.

Blossom, Ginseng, and Pebble all sniffed again around the bottom of the cliff, and then Blossom started to lead them tentatively along it.

As they walked, they passed the tree Rain and Peony had climbed. Pebble paused to sniff at it. Rain froze, holding her breath. But Pebble didn't seem to scent what had happened. He didn't look up, but instead turned away to trail after Blossom, dragging his paws through the thick ferns.

Rain waited there for several long moments, as Sunset chewed on his bamboo cane. Finally his eyes fluttered closed. She guessed that made sense—they had run all night, and the hunters hadn't had any more rest than the hunted.

She waited until she saw his big chest rise and fall with a few deep, regular breaths before she dared to move a muscle. But then she pulled back to her paws and looked around.

She wasn't sure where Peony and Shiver were, until she looked up and saw a pair of yellow eyes flashing at her through the canopy.

"Up here," Shiver whispered. "Take the left forking branch."

Rain did as she said, climbing as stealthily as she could, up along the left branch, emerging into a place with a big, solid crook where Peony was resting. From here she could see out over the forest, but not down to Sunset, which made her feel simultaneously a little safer and much more wary. They couldn't be seen, but they wouldn't know if they'd been heard. . . .

"What do we do now?" Shiver muttered.

Peony sighed. "We can't climb down while they're there."

Rain nodded. A panda climbing *up* a tree wasn't always the most graceful or stealthy of creatures—there was no way they could make it *down* to the ground with Sunset around and still have a head start when they started running again.

"I guess we wait for them to leave," she said. "Then we get their attention again somehow, to keep them following us."

Shiver settled down, spreading herself along a branch, her

tail tucked over her paws. "Then let's nap while we can," she said. She laid her head on her tail, and her eyes started to droop almost at once.

"Good idea," Rain said to Peony. "You should try to rest."

"Rain . . . ," Peony said. She wriggled a little in the crook of the tree, and Rain saw that her legs shook when she tried to put any weight on them. "If . . . if we don't move soon, if I don't find something to eat . . . I might not be able to get down again, quietly or not."

Rain took a deep breath.

"It'll be okay," she said. "I'll find something."

She turned and started to make her way back down to the lower branch.

"Rain, where are you going?" Peony breathed.

"I need to keep an eye on Sunset." Rain sighed, wishing she could stay close to her mother instead. "I'll be fine."

Peony nodded, her head moving jerkily. "Please be careful, dear cub."

Rain climbed down to the lower branch and settled there. Sunset was still resting against the next tree, his chest rising and falling slowly.

*He found bamboo right beside him,* Rain thought. *You don't get one bamboo cane by itself, not even in the Northern Forest. There must be more.*

It would be a terrible idea to climb down and try to steal bamboo from under Sunset's nose. But perhaps there was some growing a little farther away?

Well, she wasn't planning on sleeping anyway. And if she

could just bring back a few canes for Peony . . .

She nosed around at the branches, testing them with gentle pushes of her paws. She found she could pad, almost silently, along the branch from the tree she was in to the next.

It didn't take a very long time, staring around at the ground, for Rain to spot it. A clump of bamboo, seven or eight canes thick, growing at the base of a tree two or three over from hers. The canes waved in the breeze, their thin top ends laden with deliciously fresh-looking leaves.

Her own stomach rumbled, and she froze, hoping it hadn't given her away. But nothing on the ground seemed to move.

If she was going to do this, it had to be soon. Who knew when Sunset would wake up, or when the others would be back?

She walked across one more tree, stretching out to pull herself over to the next branch, and then she turned around and let herself down onto the ground, paw by paw. She peeked out from behind the tree and looked in the direction of Sunset's napping spot, but there was a tall fern spray between them now.

*Good. At least I'll have a chance.*

She loped over and stared up at the bamboo. There was no way she could get a full cane up to Peony, not dragging it through the branches, *definitely* not quietly.

She reached up and carefully, so carefully, pulled one of the canes over so that she could reach the leaves. She could pick them off, hold them tight in her jaws, and take them back up into the tree. It wouldn't be much of a feast, but it would be *something*.

Using her grip pad and her teeth, she worked as quickly as she could, bundling up leaves until she had so many she thought she'd start dropping them.

Then, suddenly, something moved overhead. Rain looked up to see what it was, and felt as if the world were slowing around her as she leaned a little too hard on the bending bamboo cane, and . . .

CRACK.

The sound seemed louder than any bamboo snap Rain had heard in her life.

Before she even had time to gasp, the ferns parted and Ginseng's large face appeared. He seemed as shocked to find her there as she felt.

"The prisoner!" he roared, and shouldered through.

There was nothing else to be done: Rain dropped the cane, dropped the leaves, and ran.

She heard more voices behind her, Blossom's and then Sunset's:

"What about the others?"

"They must have split up! Leave them! It's the lying cub I want!"

Little did Sunset know, his words sent a burst of energy through Rain's paws. *Yes. Don't look for them—follow me!*

She ran, away from the bamboo, away from the tree where Shiver and Peony must have heard what was happening. She ran, as fast as her tired paws would take her.

It was harder on her own; she wasn't as nimble as Shiver, and she tripped over ferns. She wasn't as strong as Blossom, either, and struggled around bamboo clumps that she heard her pursuers stomping straight through a moment later.

She was all alone, and if they caught her, she would be dead. And they *would* catch her before long; she had no doubt about that now. She couldn't outclimb them, couldn't outrun them.

*So much for leading him to the pool. All I'm leading him to is victory.*

The thought made her so angry, she found just a little more energy for another burst of speed, but she knew it couldn't last. . . .

Then she caught a new scent, fresh and wonderful.

*The river.*

She swerved to head straight for it.

*There is one way I might get out of this. . . .*

The trees opened up abruptly onto slippery rocks, still caked in mud and algae from a year of being underwater. Rain threw herself over them, not caring that her paws slid around under her, her eyes fixed on the surface of the water. She leaped for it, landed with an almighty splash, then took a deep, deep breath, and dived.

Under the surface, she found the peaceful world she'd visited so many times before, barely changed by the calming of the river and certainly unaware that anything dramatic was going on up above. Fish darted out of her way; weeds twisted lazily as she swam past them. She swam as hard as she could upriver, against the current, as far as she could go. Her heart was pounding. She could feel it in her eyes and her tongue, but she kept pushing until she couldn't go any farther, and then swam back to the northern shore and gently let herself rise up again.

Her head broke the surface softly, and she sucked in a deep breath through her nose. She half swam, half floated over to a tree whose roots still wound down into the river, and clung on to them while she blinked away water and peered back along the riverbank.

Four panda shapes paced the rocks where she'd jumped in, cursing as their paws slipped on the rocks. She could hear Sunset bellowing.

"Where is she?"

The four of them sniffed around the rocks and peered into the water. Rain felt a jolt of excitement as she watched them looking downstream, in the direction of the current. Just as she'd hoped.

"Dragon Speaker," she heard Pebble say in a tentative voice, "it's past the Feast of Sun Climb now."

"*So?*" Sunset snapped, turning on Pebble.

Pebble took a step backward, and Rain clutched the tree root a little harder.

*I should let Pebble get what he deserves. He's betrayed all of us. It's his fault I could get torn apart at any moment.*

*But I swear, if Sunset hurts him . . .*

"It's only . . . what will the others think?" Pebble said in a small voice. "We've vanished, and they won't know what's happening. . . ."

"Are you saying we should let the traitor get away?" Blossom snarled.

Rain's breath hitched. *Oh, Pebble. Are you trying to help us after all?*

"No, the cub has a point," Sunset said. "They should all know what danger they're in. Ginseng, go back to the feast clearing. Any panda who's strong enough, bring them to the Northern Forest. We'll cover the whole kingdom with pandas if we have to—we'll find the traitors, and we'll make sure every panda sees what happens when someone threatens their Dragon Speaker."

Ginseng bowed his head to Sunset and then set off along the riverbank, heading back toward a crossing place. Rain's blood ran cold at the idea of the Prosperhill pandas—*her* pandas, her family and friends, pandas that Peony had known all their lives—sweeping through the Northern Forest, *hunting* her.

She had to get back to Peony and Shiver. They had to get out of here and find Leaf, and *fast*.

Sunset, Blossom, and Pebble set off downriver at a run, as she had hoped they would. Pebble was the last to go, lagging behind the others. For a moment he looked down into the water, and then he turned his head to look upstream, toward Rain's hiding place. Had he known she was there all along, and hidden it from Sunset?

It was impossible to tell. A moment later he hurried on, following the others.

She waited for ten, twenty breaths after all four of them had vanished, before pulling herself up out of the water and beginning to head back inland.

It didn't take long to find her way back to the tree, to the scattered bamboo leaves. With a slightly hysterical chuckle, she scooped them up in her jaws and began to climb the tree. She only hoped that Peony and Shiver hadn't already moved on. . . .

As she passed over the second tree, there was movement in the branches above her, and she looked up, hoping to see Shiver. But it wasn't Shiver. . . .

For a horrible moment, Rain half expected to see Blossom sneering down at her, but then she realized that that was ridiculous. The thing that had moved was much smaller than a panda—it was a bird, with a long neck and long legs. . . .

*"Stick Legs?"* Rain gasped. "Is that you?"

The black-necked crane walked down the branch toward her, that same gingko-leaf-shaped red patch on its head catching the sunlight. The patch was enough, but Rain still would have been certain from the way it stared at her, dipping its neck to put its beady eyes close to hers, that this was the same bird that had saved her from falling to her death on the way back from the White Spine Mountains.

"You tried to stop me crossing the river," Rain said.

The crane said nothing—of course, because Rain couldn't

speak bird, and it couldn't speak panda—but still, the way it stared and tilted its head at her, Rain felt sure she knew what it was thinking:

*Yes, and how did that work out for you?*

"It . . . didn't go quite as I planned," Rain admitted. She took a long breath. "I have to get this food to my mother," she said. "But after that . . . how about you show me what you think I should do next?"

# CHAPTER ELEVEN

GHOST PEERED INTO THE snowstorm, planting his feet in the drifts, refusing to be moved by the howling winds. The cold seeped through his fur and bit into his skin.

*Was it always this difficult? Has living in the Southern Forest made me soft?*

It had been a long, lonely journey to the mountains. Days of climbing higher, leaving the soft earth and grass behind, feeling the air grow colder. His eye had finally reopened on the second day, after he'd started to wonder if he would be able to see through it ever again. The rest of his wounds were closing, but not yet fully healed, and the chill seemed to find its way in through every scratch on his skin, until he felt more like ice than bear.

He had slept in trees and curled behind rocks, eaten

bamboo when he could get it and fruit, nuts, and insects when he couldn't. It had been at least four feasts since he had found anything to eat at all.

*What am I doing?* he thought, and not for the first time, as he forced his way through another gust of snow to a pair of spindly pine trees and leaned against them for a moment. *Why am I doing this?*

It was all for a promise he had made to a dead tiger, for no reason other than it *felt* important. It could all be for nothing. If he didn't find the ancient stones, he would never know.

He'd started seeing landscapes he thought he recognized, places near Winter's territory that he might have visited once to practice hunting, or perhaps just passed through when he left. Everything felt smaller and bigger, all at the same time.

*I don't think I understood just how big these mountains are,* he thought. *When I was a cub, the whole world was the den, the hunting grounds, the snowfield, and the Endless Maw.*

Now he had some sense of how far these peaks went, not to mention the world beyond. And he had no idea where he could even start to search for ancient stones that looked like a tiger's eye and a panda's jaws. The tiger hadn't said how big they were, or whether they might be buried under the snow or perched on top of the peaks. . . .

He tried not to think of the sad, crumpled shape of the poor tiger, or the monkeys who had killed him.

Ghost looked behind him down the steep, snowy climb, expecting to be able to see the trail he had dug into the snowdrifts in search of these rocks, but the storm was already covering his efforts.

He shook himself, throwing off a white wave of snow, which he knew was also futile—he'd be covered again in moments.

He didn't know how he was going to do this, but obviously it wouldn't be while the storm was raging. He would have to find somewhere to shelter until the snow stopped. He stomped away from the trees, heading for the nearest high cliff, hoping there might be a cave or at least an overhanging rock where the snow was less deep and the wind less cutting.

Even when the storm ended, he knew he wouldn't be able to find these ancient rocks by digging up every patch of snow in the mountains. He would have to find help. Some creature who knew the terrain . . .

The cliff loomed out of the swirling white air in front of him, and Ghost gasped. The slope of this rock, the dark shape of the cave that was formed between giant boulders . . . it was all suddenly, intensely familiar.

It was Winter's cave. He had found his way home.

*We used to play on those little rocks beside the entrance. . . . Winter would bring prey and keep it on the high ledge just over that way. . . .*

He could almost see, in the drifting snow, the shapes of leopard cubs rolling over and over. Snowstorm and Frost, play-fighting, pretending to hunt each other around the rocks. Shiver, the smallest and weakest, always the lookout. And Ghost . . .

A little white panda cub, hopelessly out of his element,

who never understood why he wasn't good enough at being a leopard.

*But I loved my family,* he thought suddenly. *I was happy, most of the time. I learned to hunt and climb and leap as well as I possibly could have. And Winter loved me and kept me safe, even though I was nothing she'd ever seen before.*

He sat outside the cave and felt the snow piling up on his back, the weight of grief settling over him at the same time. He remembered curling up against Winter's warm belly, feeling so safe, even when he couldn't hunt or when the two bullies, Brisk and Sleet Born of Icebound, had been taunting him again.

*She gave her life for me. Just like the tiger. I owe them both. The least I can do is try to make it count,* he thought.

He sniffed at the den entrance. It smelled pretty much the same as it always had. Was someone using it as a home now?

Well, he couldn't be out in the snow much longer, either way. Perhaps whatever was inside would be willing to share its space for the night, and if not . . . he had learned to fight from the best.

As soon as he stepped inside, the familiar warm scent of leopard was almost overwhelming. There was a small tunnel, and then a larger chamber at the back—that would be where something was sleeping. He padded toward it, trying to decide whether to call out. . . .

"Who's there?" snarled a voice, and out of the darkness came two adult snow leopards. They growled at him and he backed away quickly as they crouched, ready to spring.

Then one of them stood, dropping her guard, her ears pinning back in shock.

"Ghost?" she gasped.

"*Snowstorm?*" Ghost stared at the leopard in front of him. Shiver had grown in strength and size while they'd been in the Southern Forest, but she had done it gradually, in front of him, and she'd always be smaller than her littermates. Snowstorm and Frost looked like real adult leopards, the softness around their faces turned to elegant feline features. Snowstorm looked so much like Winter, it stung Ghost's heart to look at her.

"Ghost, what in the Snow Cat's name are you doing here?" Frost said.

Ghost shrank back, suddenly remembering how they'd parted. Were they still angry with him? Would they try to drive him away?

"Never mind that now," Snowstorm mewed, and rushed toward Ghost. "He's come home!"

She hit him with such force that he sat back on his haunches, and rubbed her face against his, purring as loud as an earthquake. A moment later Frost joined them, and all three of them rolled over and over in the shed fur that lined the den, like they had when they were tiny cubs.

Ghost's heart felt like it might burst. He felt so warm inside he could have melted all the snow on the mountain with a glance. He licked his siblings all over their faces and buried his muzzle in their soft fur.

"I've missed you!" he said, only really realizing as he said it how true it was.

"We missed you too—you're so *big!*" Frost said. Ghost guessed he must have grown too—the ceiling of the den was certainly much, much closer than it had been. "You really look . . . well . . . like a bear!"

"Are you hurt?" Snowstorm said, nosing at a patch of his fur that was still slightly stained pink from a wound that hadn't fully closed.

Ghost winced. "I'm getting better. It's been . . ." He took a deep breath. How could he begin to explain to them all about everything that had happened to him in the Southern Forest? "There's a lot happening."

"Well, sit down and tell us," Snowstorm said. Ghost made himself comfortable, leaning against the smooth rock wall of the den.

"Wait—where's Shiver? Did she find you? Is she all right?" Frost yowled suddenly.

"Yes, she's fine," said Ghost. "At least, she was when I left. We traveled to the Southern Forest together."

"Oh, thank you, Snow Cat," said Frost, needling his claws in the shed fur.

"You've come a long way," Snowstorm said. "Are you hungry? Hang on."

She reared up to a high crevice at the top of the cave and pulled down a piece of prey, a hare. She dropped it at his feet and sat back, smiling.

"Thank you," Ghost said. He figured he would tell them

about bamboo later—he was starving, and this was food.

In fact, though it still wasn't ever going to be his favorite, the prey tasted a little better than he'd expected. Perhaps it was because he wasn't desperate to like it, as he'd been as a cub. He knew there were other options, foods that he was built to eat and enjoy. The hare no longer tasted of failure.

While he ate, Snowstorm and Frost told him about their lives—they had both made the jump across the Endless Maw, but then they'd heard the earth roaring, and they'd decided to stay together for the moment, rather than try to find their own territories. It was easier to hunt with two, and easier to defend their prey—there were always other creatures out to take what was left unattended, not least Brisk, Sleet, and Icebound, who were unfortunately still living close by.

Ghost took a long breath before he began to tell his story.

"I found out what I am," he said. "I'm a panda. It's a kind of bear that lives down in the south, where it's all so green, you wouldn't believe it. . . ."

As he went on, he saw the story of his life reflected on his siblings' faces—their expressions turning from awe, to joy, to suspicion and anger as he described Sunset's betrayal. Finally he told them about Brawnshanks, his unknown plans for the Broken Forest, his attack on Ghost, and the tiger that had saved him.

"A tiger," Frost breathed. "I've always wanted to meet a tiger."

"He told me there was something very important I had to

do," Ghost said. "That's why I came back. I think it has something to do with stopping Sunset and Brawnshanks taking over the forest . . . but I'm not sure how to do it."

"We'll help you," Snowstorm said at once. "Whatever it is. Oh, Ghost . . . you've had such a hard time." She lay down on her belly, her ears folding back in shame. "I'm so sorry for everything I said. When . . . when Mother died. I was horrible. I know it wasn't your fault."

Ghost shivered a little and let out a breath. He felt something lift off him, something he'd been carrying ever since he left the mountains.

"Winter would have been so disappointed in us," Frost agreed. "We drove you away, you and Shiver. Can you ever forgive us?"

"Of course. I don't blame you at all. It's forgotten," Ghost said, leaning down and giving Snowstorm a lick between her eyes. She purred at him, and shifted to sit a little closer.

"So what is it you need to do in the mountains?" Frost asked.

"The tiger said I needed to find two ancient rocks: the tiger's eye and the panda's jaws. Between them there's a tunnel, and in there I'm supposed to find a blue stone."

"And then what?" Snowstorm asked.

"I . . . I'm hoping it'll be obvious," Ghost admitted in a small voice.

"Well, the panda's jaws must be that big white rock with the jagged bits like teeth," Frost said. "Remember, Snowstorm?

We found it while we were hunting goats—I remember because it looked *weird*, like it could take a bite out of you!"

"I might know something that could be the tiger's eye, too," Snowstorm said slowly. "We'll have to go out there and find it."

Ghost felt so grateful he could barely speak. "Thank you," he said.

"But let's not go anywhere in this storm," Frost said firmly. "We can take a nap, and go out when it's calmed down."

"I would love that," said Ghost, flopping down in the nest of fur. He rested his head on the soft bed, and Frost stretched out beside him, with Snowstorm pressing in behind. Ghost almost laughed. They hadn't changed at all since they were cubs—Frost took up as much space as he physically could, while Snowstorm tried to wriggle into spaces where she absolutely wouldn't fit.

He closed his eyes, breathing in the familiar smells, listening to the sounds of his siblings breathing. . . .

And he heard voices.

All three cubs Born of Winter sat up at once, all of them hearing the growls at the mouth of their den at the same time. Frost and Snowstorm leaped to their paws and ran to the tunnel. Ghost looked past them to see two—no, three large leopard shapes barge inside, their tails swishing behind them. He didn't think they could see him, half hidden inside the cavern.

"Go away, Icebound!" Snowstorm snarled.

"Give it up, motherless cub," Icebound sneered. "We've come for your stash of prey, and we're not leaving until we get it." .

"Yeah," Brisk said. "No Winter here to defend you now!"

"Just hand it over," Icebound added, "and things won't need to get ugly this time."

*This time.* So Icebound had bullied them into letting her have their prey before? She had fought them for it—and won?

Anger flared in Ghost's heart. He stood up to his full height and stepped out into view of the three other leopards.

"What is *that?*" Sleet gasped.

"It's me," Ghost said in his deepest, most bear-sounding growl. "Don't you remember? The little white freak?" He walked forward, stepping past Snowstorm and Frost, putting himself nose to nose with Icebound. Fear flashed across the older leopard's face, and she backed away half a step. "Winter may not be here, but the cubs Born of Winter stick together!"

He opened his jaws wide and let out a growl, then reared back, raising one paw. He saw Icebound notice his claws, never retracted, long and sharp and strong. He snapped at her, missing her on purpose, and let her hear the sound of his jaws closing right by her nose, jaws that could break bamboo canes into splinters with a single bite.

"Go," Icebound yelped. Her cubs didn't need telling twice. They scrambled backward out of the cave, followed by their mother, and the snow flurries swallowed them up at once.

"Ghost!" Frost gasped. "That was terrifying!"

"It was amazing," said Snowstorm. She nudged Ghost with the top of her head. "You may be a panda, but you make a really good leopard!"

"I'm both," Ghost said. "I'm . . . me."

And for the first time, as they settled down again in the fur that smelled of home, Ghost realized that he was truly, completely happy with that. He might not fully belong either in the mountains or in the Southern Forest, but wherever he found himself next, he knew who he was. Ghost Born of Winter: part panda, part leopard, and entirely himself.

# CHAPTER TWELVE

L̲E̲A̲F̲ ̲S̲A̲T̲ ̲W̲I̲T̲H̲ ̲H̲E̲R̲ back against the trunk of the tree and her legs dangling on either side of the branch, trying to feel patient. It wasn't really working very well—she could manage little bursts of patience at a time, and then she'd find herself checking the sky again.

She had to admit, Dasher wasn't helping either—he was pacing up and down the branches, circling the tree, his long stripy tail swishing behind him as he craned his neck for any sign of birds or bats heading toward them.

All the while, Leaf kept thinking of how far a bird or a bat could travel, how quickly, and where that meant her siblings might be. What were they doing now, Rain and the mysterious third triplet? Were they all right? Were they in danger?

"Hi, Leaf," said a voice, and Leaf looked down to see Pepper sitting at the bottom of the tree. He gave her a cheerful smile. "Can I come up?"

Leaf looked at Dasher, who gave her back a look that said, *It's your choice. . . .*

"Sure," Leaf called down.

Pepper climbed up to her branch and perched beside her. "What're you doing? Are you Dragon Speaking?"

His face was so open and earnest-looking, Leaf stared at him for a moment. It was as if he'd already forgotten that she might be annoyed with him.

"Yes," Leaf said. "I hope I am. I'm waiting for news from the birds."

Pepper's eyes widened. "Wow!" He looked up at the sky, and Leaf suppressed a giggle. He looked just like Dasher. "Hey, Leaf?" he said after a while. "I know I said I'm not a Dragon Speaker, but I still *could* be your triplet, if you wanted."

Despite herself, Leaf found herself smiling at him. There was really something very sweet about the offer, as bizarre as it was. It was as if Pepper had forgotten completely that his real mother was down in the clearing, waiting to contradict anything he said. It was like if he couldn't *see* anything to contradict his stories, he didn't believe in the contradiction—or maybe he believed with his whole heart that he would be able to find a way around it later.

She couldn't find it in herself to stay angry at someone like that. His lies could definitely be destructive, and selfish, but it really did feel like he couldn't help reaching for them, even when he absolutely didn't have to.

"I don't think you need to be my triplet," she said. "I think it'd be better if you were my friend instead."

"Really?" Pepper's face lit up. "Yes, please!"

Farther up the branch, Leaf saw Dasher sigh and roll his eyes dramatically, but then he padded along the branch to Pepper's side.

"I'll be your friend too," he said.

"Yay!" Pepper got up and spun on the spot, making Leaf's stomach clench nervously as he danced worryingly close to the edge of the branch. Then he stopped suddenly and sat down hard, staring up into the sky. "Whoa. Looks like *lots* of creatures want to be friends with us. . . ."

Leaf followed his gaze, and her breath caught as she saw shapes filling the sky. Birds and bats, one by one, surging over the forest toward the Hollow Fir.

She turned and scrambled up the tree, higher and higher, holding on to the branches and leaning out until she almost felt as if she were flying alongside them.

"Have you found them?" she called. "Is there any news?"

The birds began to caw and whistle as they circled the tree, each speaking in their own way, none saying words Leaf could translate . . . and yet there was *something*. It was more a feeling than an actual sound, but she still understood it.

*Nothing,* it said. *We have not found your siblings.*

Leaf sagged, clinging on to the high, wavering branches.

"Nothing at all?" she whispered.

The message didn't change. The birds and bats started to disperse, and Leaf wanted to call them back, but she knew she couldn't—they had done their part.

She clambered back down to where Dasher and Pepper were waiting, looking expectant. Dasher's face fell as he saw her expression.

"They didn't find Rain?"

Leaf shook her head.

"I bet they got caught in a storm," Pepper said. "Or Rain was hiding so well they couldn't see her even though they looked for ages."

Leaf sighed. "We don't know why they didn't find her," she said.

"Well, we won't give up," Dasher said quickly. "Let's tell the others and come up with another plan."

"Yeah," Leaf agreed. But she didn't really feel like making another plan.

*The Dragon sent me the birds,* she thought. *It showed me I could still ask for help. I can't believe it hasn't worked. . . .*

Dasher gathered the others around and explained what was going on.

"We have to find Rain, and the other triplet," he said. "They've got to get to the Dragon Mountain, together, so they can be proper Dragon Speakers."

"We'll all help you," said Gale, stepping forward. "Between us, we can spread out pretty far."

Dasher's mother came to sit beside her. "Let's start by

searching the forest and the hills between here and the river," she said. "That way we can cover a lot of ground, but we don't have to split up too much."

Leaf's heart began to warm with gratitude as the red pandas formed up into small groups, each with a panda to lead it. Even Goji called Pepper to her, and they joined a group of Climbing Fars, though it was clear she wasn't sure exactly what was going on.

"All right," Leaf said. "Thank you, everyone. I'll go with Dasher."

Wanderer and Hunter Leaping High offered to come with her too, and they all set off, fanning out like the fronds of a fern, moving toward the river. Hyacinth, Cane, and Runner Healing Heart waited in the clearing, in case anyone came back with news or needed help.

Leaf still wasn't fully sure that this was going to help her find Rain, but it definitely helped her mood to be walking through the forest with Dasher by her side, to be doing something active, and to know that the Hollowtree pandas were all with her.

They walked to the top of a hill and looked out over the rolling crags and valleys of the Northern Forest. Leaf shivered. As far as she could see, there were forests and rocks and crevices and ponds, and the hills just kept getting taller and craggier until they turned into mountains in the far distance. . . .

She couldn't let the vast spaces frighten her, but if the

Dragon couldn't help her find her siblings, then—

A trilling cry split the air, rising above the ordinary creaking and twittering sounds of the forest. Leaf looked up, her heart pounding. A crane circled overhead, a black-necked crane with a bright red patch on its forehead. It dived past Leaf, past the Leaping Highs—who jumped in surprise—down the steep hill to land on a rock at the bottom of the next valley. It called out again and turned to look over its shoulder.

Then the ferns parted, and Leaf saw a strange creature push through the gap—a cat, not as big as Shadowhunter, but still fairly big, with very thick white fur covered in pale brown spots.

And walking behind it, supporting another panda, who was walking with a stagger . . .

"Rain!" Leaf bellowed aloud, sending several small birds scattering from the trees. Rain looked up, so surprised she almost tripped over her paws, and stared open-jawed at Leaf.

Leaf didn't wait for her to answer. She started scrambling down the slope, the three red pandas close behind her. She clambered over rocks and slid down patches of wet grass, coming to an undignified thumping stop a bear-length from Rain's nose.

"Leaf!" Rain gasped. "Thank the Dragon!" She strode forward and nuzzled Leaf forcefully under the chin. Leaf licked the top of Rain's head, startled and pleased to find her sister so affectionate.

"I'm so glad I found you," she said.

Rain nodded. "I—oh, I've got so much to tell you. . . ." She looked like she didn't know where to begin, but then she glanced back at the cat and the staggering panda behind her. "Okay, first we've got to get Peony somewhere safe," she said. "She's been starved, and we've run all the way here from the Southern Forest, basically. She's my mother—I mean, she's the panda who raised me." Rain corrected herself, looking slightly ashamed.

"Then . . . you believe?" Leaf couldn't help smiling a little. "You believe that you're my sister, that you're a Dragon Speaker?"

"Yep," Rain said, with a slightly strained smile back. "And there's a *lot* more I need to say about that too, but first . . ."

"Let's get her back to the clearing," Dasher said. He walked up to Peony and said, "Hello, I'm Dasher." Then he sniffed a little at her, and turned to look at Leaf with his ears flattening to the side of his head. Leaf's stomach lurched. If Dasher was worried . . .

"Come on," she said. "Let's get moving. You can tell me some of it on the way."

"I'll run ahead," said Wanderer. "Let Runner Healing Heart know you're coming."

They started to walk, Peony stumbling forward and leaning on the flank of the big white cat. Before they'd taken more than a few steps, Dasher crept up alongside Leaf and reared up on his back legs to put his muzzle close to her ear.

"I don't want to worry them," he whispered, "but I'm going

to go look for some purple leaf."

Leaf's stomach clenched again, and she nodded. "Thank you. Please hurry," she said.

Dasher gave her a quick nod and vanished into the undergrowth.

"We've got to be careful," Rain said, "and move as fast as we can. Sunset's in the Northern Forest, looking for me. He sent for the rest of the Prosperhill pandas to join in the search—we could be overrun with them soon. I don't suppose you've found the other triplet?"

Leaf gave a deep sigh. "I thought I had. I found this cub, and then we spent ages looking for *you* . . . it's a long story, but no. I still don't know where they are."

"Don't feel too bad," Rain said. "I didn't listen to you, and instead I tried to confront Sunset, and he threw me in a pit."

Leaf stared at her. "Maybe you'd better start from the beginning."

Rain told her about stalking Sunset, reuniting with Peony, and finally realizing that it was all true—she was a Dragon Speaker after all. Leaf gasped and winced as her sister told her about their attempt to expose Sunset's lies to the others, his deal with the monkeys, and their time in the pit. Rain described a strange white panda called Ghost, who had promised to help them escape and then didn't—and how the cat, who was called Shiver, had stayed true to her word and defended them. She spoke quickly, her eyes on the ground. When she looked up, they were full of sadness.

"And Plum?" Leaf asked shakily. "Where's Plum?"

Rain took a deep breath. "I—Leaf, I don't know how to say this.... I'm sorry.... I left her behind, but I never thought..."

Leaf started shaking her head. "No, Rain, don't..."

"I heard it when I was in the Southern Forest," Rain said. "Sunset was saying that Shadowhunter had done it, but . . . it was Sunset himself, I think. They found her by the river. Plum is dead, Leaf. I'm so sorry."

For a long moment, the entire Bamboo Kingdom seemed utterly still. Then Leaf let out a wail of sorrow and crumpled.

"Leaf," Rain was saying. "I don't want to make you move, but..."

"I know," Leaf said croakily. She sat up from where she was curled against her sister. "Sunset's on your tail, so we must keep going."

"There's something else I need to tell you too," said Rain, after they had all—pandas, red pandas, and snow leopard—started walking again. "I *did* have a vision. I saw a deep pool, like the pit, but full of water. And the water was black, or it turned black. And I saw Sunset falling into it and drowning, I think.... And now I'm *sure* I've got to get him there, or at least maybe I'm supposed to go there? I'm so sure it has something to do with getting rid of Sunset, but how am I going to find one pool of water, somewhere in the Northern Forest . . . ?"

Leaf stopped walking. "Rain, I think I might know where the pool is."

"What?" Rain stopped too, and spun to face her.

"I've seen a pool with water that turned black," Leaf said. She frowned. "It was bad water, Rain. It was poisoned or something. The Northern Forest pandas tried to make a home there, and they all got sick. Some of them almost died!"

"Sounds awful," Rain said with a hint of delight. "You have to take me there."

Leaf nodded slowly. "I think maybe we should go *now*."

Rain paused, taking a deep breath. Then she ran ahead to Peony and Shiver.

"Mother," she said softly, pressing her forehead to the older panda's. "Leaf knows where the pool is! I think . . ."

"Go," whispered Peony. Her voice was hoarse, but it was firm. "Shiver and these two fine red pandas will take me to the others. I'll be safe there."

"It's not far," Leaf said. "Wanderer, tell Runner that Dasher's gone for purple leaf, and let Hyacinth know where we've gone."

"Yes, Dragon Speaker," Wanderer said, snapping to attention.

Leaf led Rain away, heading up the slope that they'd been picking their way along.

After they'd walked a few bear-lengths from the others, Rain dipped her head and said in a soft voice, "Tell me that still feels weird to you?"

"What, creatures saying 'Yes, Dragon Speaker' and doing what I say?" Leaf said. Despite everything, she managed a smile. "Oh, *Dragon*, yes! If anything, I think it actually feels weirder the more they do it."

"Well, good," Rain said.

The Hollow Fir wasn't actually terribly far from the Dark-pool, but the closer they got, the more Leaf's fur seemed to prickle. She didn't feel entirely safe coming back here, even though she now knew that they shouldn't drink the water. As they approached the smooth, grassy, inviting-seeming hill that led down to the pool itself, she remembered rushing back with purple leaf and red-vein bamboo, hoping she wasn't too late.

"Is that it?" Rain said, breaking into a run when she spotted the pool. Leaf followed after her, anxiety shuddering under her fur.

The pool was just the same as it had been the last time—deceptively beautiful, sitting under the shade of the trees. It looked clear at first, just as it had seemed to the other pandas. The deep bottom was obscured by thriving-looking green weeds, and a few early cherry blossoms turned lazily on the surface.

Leaf glanced at Rain, who was staring down into the water with a frown on her face. She looked like she was about to say something, and then Leaf saw that blackness swirl up out of the depths, just as it had when Dasher had been about to drink from it. She took half a step back, nervously.

"Can you see it?" she asked. "Can you sense the badness in it?"

Rain was staring even harder now. "It's turned black," she said. "So that's a yes."

Leaf's hackles rose. "Don't get too close," she told her sister. "I don't know what you need to do here, but trust me, you don't want to swallow any of this stuff."

"I'll try not to," Rain said, "but I think I know what I need to do." She looked over her shoulder at Leaf and gave a nervous smile. "Be right back."

No... Leaf started forward, thinking about grabbing Rain's scruff to pull her away from the edge of the pool, but she was too late.

Rain had already dived, headfirst, into the black water.

# CHAPTER THIRTEEN

*This might have been a horrible mistake . . . .* Rain thought, but she pushed her doubts aside. Her heart had told her to jump, that there was something at the bottom she needed to see. And there was no going back now.

The black water was every bit as strange as it had been in her dream, except now it was real water, and she really couldn't breathe. She could somehow see the edges of the pond through it, the trailing roots of the plants that grew all around it. Down below her—far below, deeper into the earth than the pit had been—green weeds waved as her body moved through the water. She swam down and down, scraping the weeds aside with her paws, pushing through until her claws scraped silt and rock. The thick green leaves of the weeds parted, and there, lying in silt as black as the water around her, was something very smooth and white.

Bones. Just like in the river.

But there was something different about these bones. . . .
She pushed the silt aside, tore out weeds with her claws.

The bones in the river had been scattered, broken, small
pieces of an animal that had long ago been torn away from the
rest by the unrelenting rush of the swollen river. This was one
complete, perfect skeleton.

It was the skeleton of a bear.

Rain reached out and touched a paw gently to the bear's
skull.

The sensation that followed was as if the bottom had
dropped out of the pool and all the water had dropped
through, carrying Rain with it. A sudden rush of movement,
the water swirling around Rain, through her fur, until she
found herself abruptly above the water, gasping for air.

Her head hadn't broken the surface of the pool—she wasn't
*in* the pool at all, but sitting on a tree branch, high up in the
air. Rain made a startled noise and dug her claws into the
wood of the tree, or tried to. Something about it didn't feel
quite . . . *right*.

*This isn't real*, she thought. *This is a vision. I'm in a vision tree. Can
you fall out of a vision tree?*

She really didn't want to test it.

Carefully, she looked down. Below her, there was an eerily
familiar pool, bathed in silver moonlight. The surround-
ings were a little different, though. There was more bamboo

growing around it, a whole grove of canes, and a carpet of small white flowers that almost seemed to glow in the light of the moon. It was beautiful, peaceful-looking. And the pool itself seemed clear and inviting, even more so than it had in the real world before the blackness had overtaken it.

*This was a good place once,* she thought.

The bamboo creaked, and she saw it stir in not one place, but two—on opposite sides of the pool. She held on tight to the branch as she peered over to see who was coming.

From one side of the pool, Sunset Deepwood pushed through into the glade. Rain frowned, and looked down to see, emerging from the other side . . .

*Sunset Deepwood?*

She stared from one panda to the other, perplexed. There were two of them!

*What is the Dragon telling me?* she wondered. *That Sunset is two-faced? That he's hiding part of himself?*

"Sunset," said the one who'd emerged first. "There you are. It is good to see you again."

The second one sighed. "Brother," he said. He walked around the side of the pool and pressed his forehead to the first's. "Dusk, my dear brother. It has been a long time, hasn't it?"

"Yes," said Dusk stiffly.

Rain's neck began to tingle. Brothers! And they were so similar, far more alike to look at than she and Leaf were. She thought she had even heard something about Sunset having a brother—hadn't Sunset said he was called Dusk? Hadn't he died in the flood or something?

The two pandas sat, side by side, at the edge of the pool. Sunset looked up at the moon, and Dusk looked down into the water. The scene was peaceful, but Rain felt on edge. She couldn't help watching Sunset, waiting for him to do something awful. . . .

"It is very beautiful here," said Sunset after a while. "I'm glad you chose this place for us to meet."

He picked something up, and it glinted bright blue as he held it out. It was the same stone that he used now, to make his fake prophecies to the gullible pandas in the Prosperhill.

*The older pandas knew Sunset before the flood,* she thought. *They were so sure he was the true Dragon Speaker then. So is this what happened? Am I about to see him lose his powers?*

The stone seemed to almost mesmerize Sunset's brother. Dusk stared at it, like a hungry panda would stare at the lush bamboo that grew all around them.

"Have you heard my latest prophecy, Dusk?" Sunset asked.

"No," said Dusk. He tore his gaze from the blue stone. "I haven't. I've been on the move. What is it?"

"The Great Dragon has shown me my successor," Sunset said. His voice was soft, and he smiled sadly. Beside him, Dusk tensed. Rain saw him dig his claws into the earth beside the pool.

What was about to happen?

"Or, rather, my successors," Sunset went on. His mood

seemed to lift a little. "I am to be succeeded by three pandas—*triplets*, can you believe it? They've yet to be born, of course. News of healthy, surviving triplets would have reached us, I'm sure. They must be quite extraordinary pandas. I wish I could meet them, but . . . well, they are my successors, after all. I'm glad to have seen them, if only briefly. I'm glad I know that they will bring harmony to the Bamboo Kingdom."

He turned to Dusk, and Rain realized that Dusk's chest was heaving, rising and falling with heavy, angry breaths.

"I know why this news makes you angry," Sunset said. He sounded tired. "I know why I've been shown my successors, and why you brought me here." He got to his paws and put down the blue rock gently on a flat stone nearby. Then he turned back to Dusk. "You're going to kill me, aren't you, brother?"

Dusk didn't even speak. He simply got to his paws beside his brother, and then lunged, jaws wide. Rain cried out in horror, but the two pandas didn't seem to hear her. They rolled over in the grass, kicking and biting. Sunset was fighting back—he had one paw pressed against Dusk's flank, keeping him at a distance, and he snarled and bit at the paws that clawed at him. Rain felt dizzy as she watched them. They were almost like cubs at play, but the growling was deep and real.

Dusk pressed forward. Sunset roared a warning, but Dusk attacked again, and this time the claws in his flank tore a long, jagged wound that started to bleed profusely, a river that ran down and into the silver surface of the pond.

*I know that wound. I know the scar it left. . . .*

Rain understood, at last. Dusk raised his head and roared in pain and fury, and then pushed Sunset down, headfirst, into the pool. The moon's reflection splintered and burst as Sunset Deepwood struggled and splashed, trying to save himself as his brother held him down. Rain watched with a sob building in her chest as Dusk drowned his brother, the Dragon Speaker, just as he would later try to drown her.

Sunset went still, and Rain knew he wasn't faking it. He was dead.

Dusk let him go, and the real Sunset Deepwood slipped into the pool and was swallowed by the water.

Rain's lungs started to burn as Dusk walked away to where the blue stone had been carefully, respectfully laid down. He seized it in his jaws and turned to stomp from the glade, blood dripping from his wound.

The water from the pool rushed up, or perhaps Rain was falling down. It flowed over her head and she opened her eyes to find herself swimming in cool, clear water, her lungs burning from holding her breath too long. The blackness was gone, but the skeleton—the bones of the real Sunset Deepwood—was still there.

Rain touched her forehead to the skull.

*I wish I could have met you, too,* she thought.

Then she turned and swam for the surface, kicking with all her might. She burst out of the water with a huge gasp and threw her claws out to catch herself on the edge.

"Rain!" Leaf said. "What are you doing? You're going to make yourself sick!" She ran to Rain's side and helped her out onto the shore, yanking her by the scruff as if Rain were just a cub.

"How long . . . was I down there?" Rain panted.

"Moments," Leaf said, shaking her head. "What *happened?* You touched the bottom and the water went clear, just like that!"

"It was . . . ," Rain spluttered, trying to think of how to begin. But then she fell silent, as the undergrowth on the other side of the pool started to move and waver. Blossom pushed through, then Ginseng. And then more pandas—Crag was there, and Horizon and Yew, and Bay, and Granite. Even young Frog and his mother, Dawn, was with them, which made Rain's heart twist painfully in her aching chest. And yes, there was Pebble, too.

And leading them was a large panda, with a familiar face and a deep scar along his flank. The panda they'd all called Sunset for so long.

It was Dusk.

# CHAPTER FOURTEEN

LEAF WATCHED THE APPROACHING pandas with a growing horror. There were so many. Were these the Prosperhill pandas? Did they really mean to hurt Rain? She couldn't imagine such a thing.

"And there he is," Rain growled. She staggered to her feet, still wobbly and dripping wet from her dive. Leaf tensed, expecting to run, but Rain stood her ground and glared across the surface of the pool, regarding the leading panda with hatred through the sodden fur in her eyes. "With the big scar, you see it?"

The largest panda did have a scar along his flank, and he glared back at Rain with equal hatred. That had to be Sunset Deepwood, the fake Dragon Speaker.

Leaf felt almost as shaky as Rain seemed, looking at the

number of Southern Forest pandas who had followed him here. Even if they ran—even if Rain weren't exhausted—what chance would they have of escaping this many?

"I know how you got that scar," Rain snarled, her eyes still fixed on Sunset. "The Dragon showed me. Right here by this pool, wasn't it?"

Sunset growled, and then turned to his followers. "You see? She has lost what was left of her wits. She's a danger to herself, and to the kingdom, and she must be stopped before it's too late."

"What about the other one?" said one of the Prosperhills. She was eyeing Leaf with distrust.

"Um . . . what about *them*?" the youngest Prosperhill piped up.

Sunset looked back at Leaf, then beyond her, and his expression changed, flickering through surprise and settling on anger. Leaf looked over her shoulder and felt her fur tingle. Emerging from the trees and coming down the hill were the Hollowtree pandas and the red pandas. Some walked with purpose, some ran, and a few hung back nervously—but they had all come.

*Except . . . no Dasher,* she thought, *Or Peony, Shiver, or Runner. I hope they're all safe at the clearing. I hope Peony's all right.*

"So it's true," said Gale, stopping at Leaf's side. "Sunset Deepwood has returned—and he's turned into a fraud. Leaf and Rain are our Dragon Speakers now."

Sunset's eyes met Leaf's, and for a moment she thought he

might throw himself across the pool and attack—but then he drew himself up. "I am sorry that these two delusional traitors have drawn you into their web of untruths," he said, raising his chin to address Gale and all the Hollowtree pandas. "*I am the true Dragon Speaker, the only one.*"

"*Liar!*" Rain said. "This is *not* Sunset Deepwood."

A few of the pandas on both sides of the pool gasped, and they all stared at Rain. Leaf stared at her just as hard. What on earth had she seen in the water?

"Not Sunset?" said Juniper.

"Her story's evolving, I see," sneered the largest of the female pandas loudly. "A while ago, she was trying to convince us that he was Sunset, but he'd lost his powers somehow. This seems like the natural next step, I suppose."

Several of the Prosperhill pandas nodded grimly. But not all of them.

Rain, for her part, ignored the other panda altogether. She spoke in a loud, clear voice. "You are *Dusk*, Sunset Deepwood's brother. Sunset's bones are at the bottom of this pool. You, Dusk—*his own brother*—you wanted the stone, wanted the power and respect that he had as the Dragon Speaker. So you lured him here, and you murdered him."

The Hollowtree pandas gasped as one. They cried out, "No!" and "What in the Dragon's name?" and "How dare you!" Leaf watched the Prosperhill pandas closely. The one who had asked what to do about Leaf took a small step back from Sunset, and made sure the youngest one was close to her

side. Others moved too. They seemed uncertain what to make
of this accusation.

"There's more, isn't there?" Rain said, meeting Sunset's
eyes—

*No,* Leaf thought, *his name is Dusk.*

"I think I understand now." Rain raised her voice, address-
ing every panda, every creature within earshot of the pool, "I
can tell you why the Dragon Speaker never warned us about
the flood! Because the Dragon Speaker's death *caused* the
flood. Didn't it, Dusk? You killed him, and the act was so
terrible it disturbed the whole Bamboo Kingdom! There was
no warning, because there was no Dragon Speaker. So many
died—pandas and red pandas, and every other creature in the
kingdom. My father. Pebble's brother, Stone. So many others.
They died because of *you.*"

The horror was spreading through the Prosperhill pandas
too now. More of them were backing away from Dusk, whispering to each other. The two large pandas who'd flanked
him were drawing closer and looking around with anger and
fear in their eyes. "You were searching for the pandas who
went missing after the flood because you wanted to find me
and my siblings and wipe us out," Rain said. Leaf saw Dusk's
eyes darken and his shoulders heave as she kept on needling
him. "You made deals with the monkeys, that they'd help you
with your scheming if you made sure they got the Broken Forest all to themselves. And all to hold on to the power you stole
from Sunset—"

"And what was *he* doing with it?" Dusk roared.

An eerie silence fell over the pool as the echoes of his roar died away.

"Well? Answer me! What had Sunset ever done to deserve the power he had?" Dusk drew himself up tall again. His admission of his crime was somehow worse than if he'd tried to deny it. A light glinted in his eye now that Leaf didn't like at all.

"Sunset was always *weak*," Dusk spat. "He had the power of the Dragon in his paw, and what did he do with it? Wandered the kingdom, never took any followers or consolidated his power. He never even *tried*."

"He spoke to the Dragon," said Leaf, stepping forward. "He passed its wisdom on to the other pandas, so they could help the kingdom thrive. That's what a Dragon Speaker is supposed to do!"

"But I knew I could do so much more! I just needed this," Dusk said, and he fished in a fold of his fur and pulled out a stone. It glimmered bright blue as he held it up, and many of the pandas and red pandas gasped and exchanged glances. "This! This stone gives me authority over all of you, whether by my brother's name or my own. You will follow me, and the pandas will *rule* the Bamboo Kingdom!"

"That's not how it works," said Leaf. She didn't feel the need to shout; she knew her words would carry to all the assembled creatures without her copying Dusk's deranged tone. "Pandas aren't meant to rule. . . ." She felt a strange, unstoppable laugh bubbling up in her chest. "Pandas don't *want* to rule! We're here to guide, to *help* the kingdom. And I'm sure every panda here would rather be at home, observing the feasts and resting, than fighting for power over other creatures!"

"Nobody wants a Dragon Speaker like you," Rain spat. "Even the monkeys are just waiting for you to fail."

"Shut up!" Dusk roared. He spun to yell at the Prosperhill pandas. "Do as your Dragon Speaker says! *Kill her!*"

"You're not our Dragon Speaker," said Seeker Climbing Far.

"We should never have believed in you," added a brave young panda from the group behind Dusk. He stepped out, circling widely out of Dusk's reach, and ran around the pond to stand beside Leaf and Rain, with the Hollowtree pandas. Leaf noticed Rain giving him an intense look, while he seemed to be avoiding her gaze.

All at once, following this young panda's lead, the little cub and his mother moved too, and then more, and then *all* the pandas on the other side of the pool began to run past Dusk, all except for two thugs, who stayed put where they were, growling and snapping at those who were foolish enough to get within their reach.

"Blossom," Rain said to the large female. "You're a bully and a fool, but you can come and be a bully and a fool in peace, with the rest of us. You don't have to stay with him."

Blossom sneered and said nothing.

"Come on, Ginseng," said one of the other pandas who had

already crossed over. "I know what we talked about, but . . . he's a liar! He's not the real Dragon Speaker!"

"He's *right*, though," Ginseng snorted. "Why shouldn't we rule over the kingdom?"

"Don't bother, Ginseng," said Dusk. "Bay is as disloyal and foolish as all the others. We don't need any of them. These two impostors are still powerless. I'm still the Dragon Speaker, whether they like it or not."

"Oh, oh no! Oh dear, no!"

Every panda looked up at the sound of hooting laughter. Up in the trees, right above their heads, even though none of them had seen them arrive, dozens of golden monkeys with squashed blue faces were sitting in the branches. Now they began jumping up and down, swinging by their tails or lying in heaps against the tree trunks, helpless with laughter. It was a jarring sight, and several of the pandas growled or turned in circles to try to keep them all in sight at once.

Beside Leaf, Rain groaned.

"Hello, Prisoner," said one of the biggest monkeys, grinning cheerfully down at her.

"It's Brawnshanks," Rain whispered to Leaf. "Watch out for him. I think he might be worse than Dusk!"

"What are you doing here, monkey?" Dusk growled.

Until that moment, Leaf had hardly seen a flicker of uncertainty cross Dusk's face. But now, as he looked up at the monkey leader, his anger suddenly seemed much less controlled.

"Oh, we weren't far away," Brawnshanks chuckled. "And we had to come and witness this sorry sight. Not very popular, are you, Dusk?"

"I don't need their approval," Dusk snarled.

"No," Brawnshanks said. He hopped down to a lower branch, swinging wildly by one arm, then by his tail. "I suppose you think you just need . . . *this*?"

He dropped out of the tree, straight down, past Dusk's paw, and then in a flash he was gone from Dusk's reach and back up in the tree.

And he was holding the blue Dragon Speaker stone.

A chorus of gasps and cries of *no* and *stop* ran through the crowd of pandas, but not one of them was quick enough to prevent him.

"Why *this*?" Brawnshanks wondered, tossing the stone from paw to paw. "I've never understood what does this actually *do*? I suppose you wouldn't know, though, would you, not being a real Dragon Speaker and everything."

Leaf saw one of the other monkeys climbing along the branch toward Brawnshanks. It was also holding something in one of its paws, striking the branch with it as it walked. It was a large black rock.

She knew what was about to happen.

She didn't have time to say anything, not even to Rain. She ran for the nearest tree and threw herself up it, paw over paw, pushing herself harder than she had before. She landed hard on a branch, making it bow and creak, but she couldn't stop.

If she jumped to the next tree, she could run around, she *might* make it before . . .

"Nice try," Brawnshanks said, looking right at her. And he tossed the blue stone to the monkey with the rock, who caught it, laughed, and brought the black rock down hard on the stone.

The blue stone shattered, crushed against the tree branch. Shards of it, barely more than dust, rained down over Dusk's head, and he screamed in frustration, while below Leaf's feet the pandas gasped and cried out in shock.

"Go back to your territories," Brawnshanks declared, gathering up a fistful of the sparkling blue fragments. "Go back to eating and sleeping, like good pandas, and forget all about this. You won't need it. Now there will be no more Dragon Speakers. *Ever!*"

# CHAPTER FIFTEEN

*Here I am again,* Ghost thought, *trying to help while my siblings do what they're good at. . . .*

But the feeling didn't sting the way it used to. Now he was simply grateful to have them, with their big, agile paws. They were clearing away the snow at the base of a cliff, digging through it with a speed that Ghost couldn't have matched no matter how hard he tried.

The morning was bright, but still freezing. The storm had died away, but snow still drifted through the air, enormous flakes that landed and melted on Ghost's nose.

Snowstorm's whole front half was in the hole they were digging now, and Ghost wondered if she could really have seen the stone they were looking for if it was this far underneath the snow. If she saw it in the middle of summer, perhaps . . .

Then he heard a scrape of claws on stone that made his fur tingle, and Snowstorm made a triumphant yowl and jumped down with all four paws into the hole.

"This is it!" she said. Both Ghost and Frost stood back as she worked with her front and back paws, throwing more snow aside, finally shoving a chunk of it with her shoulder so that it cracked and fell over. She turned around and around, sweeping the surface of the rock with her tail, and then leaped out onto the snow to stand beside Ghost, panting happily.

Ghost looked down and caught his breath.

There was really no mistaking it: The rock was a bright yellow, smooth on the surface but mottled through with amber cracks and veins. Ghost realized he had occasionally seen shards of this kind of rock lying around the mountains, but never one so huge and perfect—except for a long crack right down the middle that had filled with small black stones.

"The tiger's eye," he said. "It's exactly right. This is it."

"I knew I'd seen it," Snowstorm said, licking her paws smugly.

"Let's go," Frost said. "I'll show you the thing I think might be the panda's jaws. Then we can start looking for this tunnel of yours!"

He trotted across the snow, and Ghost turned to follow him, Snowstorm bringing up the rear, her tail curling happily.

It was good to be out with his siblings again, and this time with no feeling that he was getting things wrong all the time.

He could appreciate their grace in the snow, the way that Frost seemed able to navigate by the slightest hints of what lay underneath. He explained as he went: A branch stuck up here indicated where, in the summer, stood a bush or a tree. A dip in the snow told him that when the snow melted, there was a ditch where the water ran down and made a stream. Finally he came to a spot where a white rock jutted up out of the snow, and stopped.

"This is it!" he said.

Ghost peered at it. It was just an ordinary rock, sticking out from the side of a cliff.

"You'll see," said Snowstorm, and the two leopards started to dig again.

This time, it was obvious after only a moment that the rock was more than it seemed. One, then two, then several cracks appeared as they dug down, and those cracks turned into jagged shards of rock that seemed to hang from the bottom of the white stone. Frost and Snowstorm kept digging out the hole underneath the rock until Frost yelped—he'd caught his paw on another rock, sticking up out of the snow underneath.

"It's all right," Ghost said. "You don't have to keep digging—I can see it."

The hole in the middle of the rock gaped like a roaring mouth surrounded by sharp teeth.

"It's definitely *something's* jaws, anyway," said Frost, hopping backward and licking at his paw.

"Hey, Ghost eats trees now," said Snowstorm, nudging

Ghost's shoulder with her own. "And no wonder he does, with jaws like this!"

Ghost grinned and nudged her back. He stared at the rock jaws, open and roaring out from the side of the mountain.

"The tiger called this the Dragon Speaker," he muttered. "And the other one he said was the Watcher. And exactly between the two . . ."

He looked back. He could still see the prints they had left to come here from the Watcher—especially his—but they vanished around the corner of a hill.

"Snowstorm," Frost said, his ears pricking up, "You run back to the tiger's eye. Ghost and I stay here. Then we both start walking toward each other. We should meet in the middle, right?"

"Frost, that's a great idea," Snowstorm said. "But how will I know when to start walking?"

"I'll shout," said Ghost. The others looked at him warily.

"Think you can roar loud enough?" Frost asked.

"But *not* so loud you cause an avalanche?" Snowstorm added quickly.

"It'll be fine. Trust me," said Ghost, with a little more confidence than he really felt.

Snowstorm set off, and Ghost and Frost waited, Ghost stamping his paws in the snow, trying to remember how far it was back to the tiger's eye stone. At last he looked at Frost, and Frost nodded.

"I think so, yeah."

"All right." Ghost took a deep breath and cast one last look at the white rock panda's jaws. Then he opened his own jaws and let out a barking roar. Frost jumped as the sound vibrated the air around them, echoing from the peaks of the mountains.

They both paused a moment, looking up at the snow piled up on the cliffs over their heads, holding their breath. But the snow stayed where it was.

"Go, go!" Ghost urged, and Frost scrambled past him and started walking. Ghost trailed after him as he stepped deliberately across the snow, following the line of the cliff as it zigzagged in and out, sloped away to a gentle hill, and then returned to a steep climb dotted with snow-covered bushes. Suddenly Snowstorm emerged around the corner, and they walked toward each other with deliberate steps, until they bumped noses.

"Here somewhere, then?" Snowstorm said, looking up at the steep slope.

Frost sniffed around the edges of a bush that seemed to be growing out of the side of the hill, not up through the ground. He started digging, and Snowstorm and Ghost both joined him, Ghost scraping the snow back with his claws. They uncovered the roots of the bush, wrapped around and through the cracks in the rock, and then the crack underneath it grew wider and deeper. . . .

"I think this is it!" Snowstorm said, sticking her nose right into the hole. "I can feel air moving!"

They dug harder, and the hole grew bigger, until Ghost's claws suddenly met no resistance but cold air. He scraped out more and more snow, until he could peer inside.

The tunnel entrance was small, and still partially full of the snowdrift that had piled up in it during the storm. The space on the other side was pitch dark, and smelled of almost nothing, just snow and wet rock. It looked a little like a path of white snow that led down into empty space. Apart from a faint sense of cold air, there was no way to tell how far the tunnel went.

"And . . . what is it you're supposed to do in there again?" Frost asked a little nervously, poking his nose in beside Ghost's.

"Find a blue stone," said Ghost, pulling back. "Save the Bamboo Kingdom."

"In . . . the dark?" Snowstorm asked.

Ghost didn't quite know what to say. He hadn't thought of that.

"And how is a stone supposed to save the kingdom?" Snowstorm added.

"I . . . don't really know," Ghost admitted. "But I do know that the tiger's been right so far. I think I have to do this." He turned to Snowstorm and then Frost, nuzzling each of them in turn. "Thank you so much," he said. "I would never have gotten this far without you. You don't have to come in here with me."

"Well, *obviously* we're coming," Frost said. "We just want to be prepared."

"But since it looks like we're *not* prepared," Snowstorm said, "shall we get on with it?"

"I'll go first," Ghost said, scraping out even more snow until there was a gap he could wriggle through. He found himself sliding gently down the snowdrift, down and down into the darkness, until his paws found cold, damp stone. The darkness became total as the opening was blocked by Frost and then Snowstorm slipping in after him, and he shuffled forward, feeling along the ground with his paws, moving slowly in case he walked straight into something.

But there was nothing in front of him, not for five paw steps, then ten, then twenty. The tunnel was close on both sides—he could feel the rock walls brushing against his fur—but for a while he thought it might go right through the mountain, or down to the bones of the earth.

Then, so gradually he wasn't sure exactly when he'd noticed it, he started to be able to see. First in deep grays, but then suddenly he could clearly see his paws in front of him, and then the end of the tunnel.

"I can see . . . something," Ghost said.

He didn't want to say any more, though he pressed on, his heart in his mouth. He thought he must be imagining things. Perhaps it was because he'd been in darkness for a while. Surely the colors he was seeing beyond the tunnel couldn't be real.

But they were.

The tunnel emerged onto a wide rock ledge of the greenest

stone Ghost had ever seen, overlooking a cavern and an underground pool. And every inch of the rock was bright with color. The ceiling was a bright, summer-sky blue. Stalagmites and stalactites grew from the floor and the ceiling, each one a clumsy, chaotic mix of colors. Light shone through jagged cracks in the ceiling and hit the still surface of the underground lake, scattering reflections of rainbow light all around the cavern.

"*Whoa!*" Frost said as he stepped out onto the ledge beside Ghost. His voice echoed for what felt like a very, very long time. "I mean, wow," he whispered after it had stopped. Even the whisper seemed to carry across the lake and come back to him on the cold air.

"This is . . . ," Snowstorm began, but then she just stopped, shaking her head. Her wide eyes flashed with reflected color as she took it all in.

"There's a lot of blue stone in here," murmured Frost. "Can you just take any of it?"

Ghost walked to the end of the ledge and discovered that it sloped down into a rough, rocky path that ran around the edge of the pool. He walked up to a piece of the rock wall that was bright blue, and sniffed it, and then touched it with his paw.

It was rough to the touch, like ordinary rock.

"I . . . I think I'm looking for something smaller. And smooth," he said. "Like the Watcher stone."

"Then let's start looking," said Snowstorm.

They moved around the cavern, picking their way across

the rocks. Snowstorm walked her front paws down a near-vertical spine of rock to get close to the water, and then pulled back, her whiskers dripping. Frost hopped up onto a flat column that looked like a stalagmite with the top section broken off. It wobbled wildly and he hopped off again.

"Careful," Snowstorm yowled.

"Hey," Ghost said. He had followed the flattest, easiest path around the pool, knowing that his leopard siblings would be able to climb over the more difficult rocks, and he suddenly felt air blowing in his fur. He peered around a large rock and found himself looking at a second, even larger cavern. "There's more to this place," he called over his shoulder as he stepped across the rocks, from green to purple to red and back to blue, and into the next cave.

The water ended in a shallow rocky cove, and beyond it the caverns grew much darker, though still bright enough for him to pick his way across the ground, and the colors still took his breath away. He sniffed into the corners as he walked, touching his paws to the sides of the stalagmites, hoping to find smooth, loose stones.

Snowstorm padded past him. He recognized the look on her face—she was following a scent.

"What is it?" he asked.

"Shh!" Snowstorm's ears were twitching. Ghost stopped walking and held his breath, watching them. Suddenly they swiveled, and Snowstorm pointed her nose toward something that Ghost couldn't smell or hear.

"Something is moving," she murmured, when Frost had joined them. "Something is in here with us."

Ghost's head snapped up and he stared into the darker end of the cave. Rocks stood out from the walls at jagged and strange angles—behind each one there could be a creature lurking, or an opening into another part of the cavern.

"We stick together," he whispered.

They pushed on, the three of them padding as stealthily as they could, Snowstorm and Frost moving so quietly that Ghost would barely have known the leopards were beside him except that he could hear their soft breathing along with the quiet click of his own claws on the stone. They still sniffed and peered at the walls, Ghost trying to look for a blue stone without taking his eyes off the shadows against the colored walls for more than a heartbeat at a time. Sure enough, behind one of the rocks he found another opening, this one smaller and darker still, but leading into another wide, dim cavern. There was a scent all of a sudden, strong enough for Ghost to pick up, but he couldn't identify it, except that yes, it was a creature. Something in there was alive. . . .

But he had to keep looking. He swallowed and crept through, hunched and prepared to flee, peering into the darkness.

Was that a voice he heard, whispering something, echoing back from the jagged purple rocks? What were those strange moving shadows on the floor?

All of a sudden, a rattling sound burst around him, and a

wailing sound came with it: a cry of fear that chilled Ghost down to his bones.

And then he stood up straight, relief running through him like a clear mountain stream, sweeping away his fear.

"It's a herd of goats!" he said.

They were pressed against the wall, stamping their hooves—that was the rattling noise—and braying in fear at the sight of Ghost. Their long fur and curling horns caught a shaft of light from right above them and cast strange shadows over the rocks every time they moved.

"What?" Snowstorm stuck her head through the opening, and the goats let out another collective cry of terror.

"Please!" they brayed. "Don't hurt us! Mercy!"

"It's all right!" Ghost said, standing back a few paces. "We're not here to hurt you!"

The goats went quiet, but almost as one they turned suspicious yellow eyes on Snowstorm and Frost. Ghost couldn't blame them, not one bit. It must be terrifying to be trapped in a small cavern with two predators and a big white creature they'd probably never even seen before.

"I promise you," he said. "My name is Ghost. I'm a panda—we don't eat goats; we're plant eaters, just like you! What are you doing in here?"

"W-we came in to shelter from the storm," bleated one of the goats. "Oh, please don't let those leopards eat us!"

"I won't, I promise," Ghost said, turning to look at Frost and Snowstorm.

Frost sniffed. "They are prey, though," he muttered. "What if we just took one?"

"*No*," Ghost hissed, as a quiet bleating of distress rose from the goats again. "No, that's not going to happen. Look. You two, move right over there and stay by the wall." He gestured with his nose to a dark nook to the right of the entrance. Snowstorm and Frost slunk around behind him, pressing themselves to the wall. "The storm's not so bad now, and we've dug out the tunnel entrance," Ghost said. "You should be able to get out."

He stood aside, and the goats bolted for the exit, their hooves clattering and slipping on the damp stone.

"Thank you," quavered the last one, turning to Ghost as she passed, before prancing after the others as quick as her stiff legs would take her. Ghost watched them go, and let out a small chuckle at himself for being so afraid of creatures who were *much* more scared of him.

"Ghost," said Snowstorm in a strange, quiet voice.

"You couldn't have taken one of them anyway," he said, turning back to look at her. "It would have been chaos. . . ."

But then he saw that she and Frost were both staring over his shoulder.

"Look," Frost said.

Ghost turned to look at the wall where the goats had been, and gasped.

The rough green-and-purple rock was shot through with a glinting, glittering seam of blue stone, as wide as Ghost's leg.

It swirled and twisted through the wall, coiling like a snake—but not entirely like a snake, Ghost thought. A few shorter seams broke off from the larger one, so it looked like a snake with four clawed feet, almost like a bird's, and a head with open jaws and trailing whiskers that strangely reminded him of the tiger.

"What *is* it?" Snowstorm asked. "It is a creature, isn't it? You two can see it too?"

Ghost stared in silence at the blue stone for a moment longer. "I think it's the Great Dragon," he whispered. He tried to remember how the Prosperhill pandas had described it. They had recounted vague, contradictory-seeming stories passed down from panda to panda, as if they were talking about a real creature that had last been seen many generations ago. After all, how could one animal be as long as a snake, but with a cat's muzzle, clawed feet, and fur along its back? How could it fly with no wings and swim with no gills?

But this shape fit the descriptions exactly. It was too specific to be an accident, and that meant . . .

"It's real," Ghost whispered, in awe. "It must be, this is . . . this is amazing."

"What's a dragon?" Snowstorm said. "I mean, apart from *that.*"

"It's like the panda version of the Snow Cat," Ghost said. "They ask it for help and thank it for their meals."

He approached the dragon seam, awe filling his chest.

"And this is the stone, right?" Frost said. "It's got to be."

"Oh yes." Ghost put his nose right up to the smooth stone and sniffed it. "But I . . . I have no idea how I'm supposed to take some of it away from here."

He leaned forward, and with the greatest reverence he could muster, nudged the surface of the stone with his nose.

Something struck him on the head, and he recoiled with a yelp. The thing bounced off and struck the floor, then rolled to a stop by his paw.

"Snow Cat," Frost whispered. "That was lucky!"

Ghost looked down, wincing from the bump to his head, and saw a smooth, round, blue stone.

"It fell right out," Snowstorm said. "It used to be one of the claws, look!"

Ghost picked up the stone in his paw, using his grip pad to hold it like he'd hold a piece of bamboo. It was surprisingly heavy, and as he rolled it, he thought he saw flashes of other colors inside it, though it seemed as if they appeared in different places each time he moved it. Was it just reflecting the stones of the cavern?

"It's like the cave's helping you," Frost said. "First the goats are in here to catch our attention, and now this?"

"What do we do now?" Snowstorm asked.

"I guess I have to take this . . . somewhere," Ghost said. "I think we can leave this place now."

He picked up the stone in his jaws. How did Sunset carry his around? He found that he could slip it into his cheek, like he'd seen squirrels in the Southern Forest do with their food, and it would sit there fairly comfortably. He just hoped he didn't accidentally swallow it—he was pretty sure that was not part of the tiger's plan!

They made their way back through the cavern, the light and colors brightening as they returned to the underground lake. Ghost looked around at the bright walls and promised himself that he wouldn't ever forget this place. It was like nothing he had ever seen before.

"We have to bring Shiver here one day," he said. He felt a pang of worry, but he pushed it aside.

The goats must have strayed into the water, or maybe kicked some loose stones in, because as Ghost and his siblings circled the pool, its surface was broken and rippling, casting dancing reflections of light all around the cavern, like white shadows. He followed the movement, and saw something out of the corner of his eye that seemed strange, different. . . . It was brilliant white, but faint at the same time, and it didn't move like the reflections. It moved like . . .

Like a long leopard tail, swishing and curling as it vanished around a rock.

He hurried after it, around the corner to a place where he could look up at the dark tunnel entrance they'd come through.

Then he froze, his breathing catching in his throat. He knew that outline, that movement. He watched the bright leopard shape vanish into the tunnel, and his jaw fell open, the blue stone clattering to the ground.

"*Mother?*" he gasped.

"What?" Frost skidded up to him and looked up too, and so did Snowstorm. He felt their quick breathing and their lashing tails beside him, but . . .

"Ghost, what are you looking at?" Snowstorm asked.

"She was here," Ghost whispered. "She went . . ."

He didn't stop to explain it. He *couldn't* explain it. He just knew that he had to follow her. He rushed up onto the ledge and squeezed into the tunnel, running full speed into the darkness. With no fear of falling, it seemed a lot shorter, only a few bear-lengths before he saw a flash of bright white in front of him. Was it the leopard, or the snow outside the tunnel mouth? He wasn't sure. He scrambled up the snowdrift and out into the open air.

White flakes swirled all around him, soft and huge and bright white. He looked around, his heart squeezing painfully. Was he too late? Was she gone?

No . . . she was right in front of him. In the strange daylight, in the snow, Winter looked even more real than she had in the cave. She sparkled faintly, like snow under sunlight. She looked right at him, with white eyes that he thought saw through him to his heart, saw everything he had been through. She blinked softly and smiled.

But she wasn't alone. Emerging from the air, flanking Winter, were two other figures. They were both adult female pandas, both the same shining, fresh snow-white that she was, but with patches of rich black. He didn't want to take his eyes off his mother, but he stared at the two pandas. He realized with a jolt that one of them was Plum. She still bore the scar across her face, the one he'd given her, shining like a vein of frozen ice. But she didn't seem angry. She smiled and looked at the other panda.

Ghost didn't know her. She was a little younger than Plum. She stepped forward to stand beside Winter, and they looked at each other with a fond kind of understanding. Then all three of them turned, and in the direction they were gazing, the snow parted. Ghost saw a glimpse of the landscape behind the storm: clear sky and a vast purple mountain wreathed in mist.

The snow began to close over them again. Winter looked back at Ghost once more, and then all three of them started to walk away.

"No, wait, Mother, wait!" Ghost tried to chase after them, but the snow swallowed them up, and no matter how he ran and called, Winter was gone. There was no response but the howling wind.

He fell down on his belly in the snow, bereft and confused, his heart aching.

"Ghost!" Snowstorm came bursting through the snow to his side, with Frost close behind her. "Are you all right? What's going on?"

"I saw her," Ghost wailed. "I saw Mother—she was right here!"

"Oh, Ghost." Snowstorm lay down beside him, her soft fur

warming against his, and groomed the side of his face. "I'm sorry. . . . Mother's gone, forever."

"I know," Ghost said in a small voice. "She's dead. I know. But I *saw* her. . . ."

"Didn't the Snow Cat send you a vision once?" Frost asked. "I know we were a bit skeptical at the time, but . . ."

"Yes," Ghost whispered. He nuzzled Snowstorm for a moment, and then got to his paws. "She . . . she wasn't alone. There were two pandas with her. One of them I knew; she . . . she's dead too."

His mind was spinning. The Snow Cat's vision had been incredible, but nothing like this. . . .

Frost leaned down and dropped the blue stone from his jaws into the snow in front of Ghost's paws. Ghost looked at it, and the world seemed to stabilize. He felt he could focus again. He looked up, straight ahead, and though he saw nothing but the swirling snow, he knew what he was facing toward.

"I know what I need to do next," he said. "That's why she came. Mother showed me where I need to go. I need to take the stone to the purple mountain."

# CHAPTER SIXTEEN

RAIN STOOD AMONG THE stunned pandas, her mouth hanging open, as the sound of the monkeys' laughter filled the Northern Forest.

*What has Brawnshanks done?*

The monkey leader brushed the last shards of the crushed stone off the tree branch, cackling and looking down at Dusk.

"What a fool!" he crowed. "To think you could outwit us! To think the monkeys of the Broken Forest would ever allow you to go on ruling over this kingdom!"

The other monkeys shrieked and pointed their long fingers at Dusk, who was shaking with barely suppressed rage.

*I knew the monkeys were manipulating him . . . but they've broken him, more effectively than I could ever have hoped to do.*

"You've turned your own pandas into your enemies,"

Brawnshanks sneered. "Well done, Dragon Speaker! And now we must leave you. We have bigger concerns. Feel free to destroy yourselves!" He gave a sweeping, mocking bow, and the monkeys sprang away, hooting and shrieking, scattering among the trees and vanishing in moments.

A deathly silence fell over the clear pool. Blossom and Ginseng regarded Dusk nervously as he bent down slowly and touched his paw to the pile of dust and shards that had been Sunset's stone.

Leaf slid to the ground and sat there at the base of the tree, seeming too shocked to move.

Frog was the one who broke the silence.

"What will happen without the stone?" he whispered to Dawn, patting her arm anxiously.

"We don't know," Yew replied.

And then all the pandas seemed to be talking at once.

"What did it do? What was it for?"

"Will we ever hear from the Dragon again?"

"Will there be another Speaker?"

"What will he do?"

Rain kept her eyes focused on Dusk. She took another step forward, and didn't raise her voice, but spoke directly to Dusk across the pool.

"That was *mine*," she said. "Mine and my siblings'. And it's your fault it's been destroyed. If you hadn't had to cover up your fakery, if you hadn't killed your brother, the monkeys never would have gotten their fingers on the stone, or on the

Broken Forest. Whatever happens next—whatever Brawn-shanks is planning—I hope you remember that you did this."

The pandas had fallen quiet to listen. Dusk turned his bloodshot eyes on her. He raked the ground with his claws.

"Rain's right," said Leaf, standing beside her. "You'd better leave, Dusk. We don't want you here."

One of the Northern Forest pandas spoke up. "That's right."

"You lied to all of us," said Crag.

"Get lost," said Pebble, quietly coming to stand beside Rain. "Before you hurt anyone else."

Dusk snarled. Then he sputtered a bitter, angry laugh. "You'll all regret this," he choked. "You, Rain—you most of all. I'll make you suffer for this."

Rain shook herself, sending droplets of water flying, and then slowly walked forward, circling the pool, moving toward Dusk. "Yeah?" she said. "With all these pandas at my back, you still think you can threaten me?"

She felt Leaf and Pebble fall in behind her, and saw from the corner of her eye as the Northern and Southern Forest pandas, and their red panda friends, began to walk around the other side of the pool. Blossom and Ginseng stood on either side of Dusk, growling at the advancing pandas. They were *still* standing their ground. The stupidity of it!

Rain saw red, and with a yell she charged. And she wasn't alone. She felt the ground shake beneath her paws as the pandas surged forward. She reared, aimed a slash of her claws across Blossom's nose, and braced herself to dodge Blossom's snapping teeth at her throat—

But Blossom reared away. Ginseng, too, his gaze flicking wildly between the oncoming pandas. Rain's claws passed harmlessly through the air and struck the damp earth at her paws.

Both of Dusk's thugs backed off, furiously growling but unwilling to fight every other panda in the kingdom, not to mention the red pandas, who were climbing the trees and weaving between the paws of the pandas, their small jaws full of sharp teeth snapping at Blossom's and Ginseng's ankles.

Rain roared after Blossom as she backed away. Blossom gave one last roar in response, and then she turned and fled.

Rain met Dusk's eyes, as both his most loyal pandas turned tail and ran. He held her gaze for a moment, his breath coming slow and heavy through his muzzle. She felt as if he was repeating his promise, silently, just to her: *I'll remember you. You'll still suffer for this.* It made her fur twitch as a chill passed through her, from her paws to her tail.

But she shook it off.

*Remember me as the one who beat you,* she retorted in her mind, and surged toward him.

Dusk ran. He turned and pounded into the trees after Blossom and Ginseng, barging through a cluster of bamboo canes, leaving them broken in his wake.

The pandas gathered around Rain, looking into the forest.

"Should we try to go after them?" asked Wanderer, the red panda.

"No," Leaf answered. "Let them go. Now that everyone knows the truth, I don't think we'll see him again."

Rain threw Leaf a skeptical glance. She wasn't sure of that at all. But she decided not to voice her worries, not right now.

A sigh of relief was passing through the pandas at the thought that Dusk's reign was over and done with, but several of them had gathered around the crushed blue stone, too, sniffing at it and searching for any shards large enough to pick up.

"What *does* it mean?" asked Crag.

"Rain, you told Dusk that this was yours," said Yew. "And your siblings'. But what did you mean? You don't have any siblings!"

"Ah . . ." Rain looked at Leaf. "Actually . . . this is my sister, Leaf. Our mother was Orchid. Peony will tell you—she's with the red panda healer right now. We're two of triplets, though our third sibling is still missing. And . . . we're your new Dragon Speakers."

She suddenly wished that Shadowhunter were here right now—it all sounded much more believable coming from the mouth of a giant predator.

"Hold up your paw," Leaf said, nudging Rain and holding hers up. Rain did the same, letting everyone see the pure white grip pad they both had.

"Could be a coincidence . . . ," said a skeptical voice

"Have you ever seen one like it before?" demanded one of the Northern Forest pandas. "Have you ever heard of triplets surviving? And they've both had visions from the Dragon."

"I saw Sunset Deepwood," Rain said. "The real one. I touched his skeleton at the bottom of the pool, and I saw a vision of Dusk killing him. And he said that the Dragon Speaker after him would be triplets. And that he wished he could have met them," she added, turning to Leaf.

"I wish that too," said Leaf softly.

"But . . . *Rain?*" she heard Horizon whisper to Yew. "Are you *sure?* She's not . . ."

Rain almost laughed. She couldn't really blame Horizon for wondering if she was Dragon Speaker material. She'd wondered the same thing.

*But it seems like I don't get much choice in the matter, and neither do you.*

"Leaf and Rain have our support," said one of the red pandas, stepping forward. "There's no point arguing that. The question is, will they ever be able to speak directly to the Great Dragon, without the stone?"

Rain felt as if she'd walked out on a patch of grass and discovered it was green algae over deep water. Now that Dusk was gone, now that the immediate danger had passed, she realized that she had begun to *want* to be a Dragon Speaker, to actually hear the voice of the Dragon. And if that was what the stone was for, and the stone was gone . . .

"Maybe we can find another one," Leaf said quietly. "Maybe we can ask the Dragon where Sunset got his?"

Rain nodded, but she could tell that Leaf was just trying to make the best of it all.

"We'll figure something out," she said.

"I . . . I guess we should go back to the Prosperhill," said Granite.

"Rain," said a Northern Forest panda, "I'm Crabapple. You said that the real Sunset's bones lie at the bottom of this pool?"

"Yes," Rain said. "I can dive back in and try to clear the weeds more, if you want to see. . . ."

"It's not that," Crabapple said. He turned to all the other pandas. "Before the Southern Forest pandas return to their territory, I think we should mourn and celebrate Sunset Deepwood, the last Dragon Speaker, as we do all pandas who leave us."

"Yes," said Bay. "Let's feast together."

"Come back to the Hollowtree clearing," Leaf said. "We'll gather the bamboo and have it there. Then you can all see Peony, too."

Rain's heart sped up a little at this mention of her mother, and she started in that direction at once, trusting that most of the others would follow her—though she had to slow down to let a Hollowtree panda who actually knew the way get to the front of the group.

It felt good to be moving through the forest without Dusk on her tail, surrounded by her own family and Leaf's. They were all starting to talk, sharing tales of who they had been before the flood, places they'd lived, and pandas they knew in common.

Rain and Leaf stuck together. Rain was slightly shocked to discover that even though they'd spent most of their time as sisters separated, and even more of it arguing with each other, Leaf was the one panda here—apart from Peony—she felt the closest to.

"Rain?"

She looked around to see Pebble making his way toward them. He hung back, looking at her shyly, until she nodded and he came up to walk by her side.

"I don't know how I can apologize," he said.

"How about starting with *sorry*?" Rain retorted.

"I'm so sorry!" Pebble cried. "I was so confused—well, no, not confused, I was just stupid. We all were."

Rain sighed. "It was *awful*, Pebble. I thought you were the one panda I could always trust to believe me."

"I know." Pebble hung his head.

"But he had all of you fooled," Rain added. "Even Peony, for a bit. I guess I can't blame you for getting sucked in when everyone else was too."

"Except you," Pebble said. "You were onto him, right from the beginning, weren't you? No wonder you're a Dragon Speaker."

"Well, I'm not quite yet," Rain said, trying to look stern, though deep down his words warmed her heart. He'd seen what she was going through. He just hadn't understood it until now. Perhaps that was forgivable. "Sunset—the real Sunset—said his successors would be triplets, and I have to believe our other sibling is still out there, somewhere. We have to find them." *And then there's the stone,* she added to herself.

Then they pressed through a patch of ferns, and Rain found herself looking at a pleasant clearing surrounded by bamboo glades and tall pine trees, and there, by a small stream on one side of it, were three creatures. She broke into a run, pounding across the grass to Peony's side, her heart in her mouth. But before she'd even gotten there, her mother lifted her head and smiled. Shiver sat proudly beside her, her tail swishing.

"She's doing well," she told Rain.

"Feeling much stronger," Peony said, and tried to get to her paws, but Runner Healing Heart put a paw on her head to keep her lying down.

"You still need rest," he said. Peony lay back with a soft smile at Rain.

"Dusk is done," Rain said, and when Peony frowned, she corrected herself. "Oh, *Sunset*—except he's not really Sunset; he never was! He was Sunset's brother, Dusk, and . . . I'll tell you the whole story later," she said, at a slight glare from Runner. "But it's over—we're safe. For now."

"Peony, I'm so glad you're all right! Where's Dasher?" said Leaf, trotting up beside Rain.

Peony and Shiver gave Leaf slightly blank looks, and Runner frowned.

"Dasher wasn't with them," he said.

Rain saw Leaf's ears twitch with worry. "No—he went to find some purple leaf," she said. "He hasn't come back yet?"

"No," said Runner.

Leaf sagged. Then she shook herself and gave them a smile. "Well, I'm sure he'll run in any minute with his jaws full of purple leaves. It's just a shame. He wouldn't want to miss Sunset's feast as well as everything else. . . ."

"Come on," Rain said. "Let's go and help gather the bamboo for the feast."

The other pandas were already piling bamboo around the biggest rock in the clearing. Rain had only seen a death feast shared once before, when old Clay, Mist's mate, had died. The rock stood in for the panda, the feast of bamboo supposed to be one last meal shared with their family, to see them on their way to the stars. Rain hoped that Sunset had made it to the stars long ago, but she thought it would have made him happy to see pandas from all over the kingdom coming together like this, to say goodbye to him.

Rain broke off jawfuls of bamboo canes and stacked them with the others, until the boulder had vanished under a thick, lively spray of green. An ache squeezed her heart as she saw Leaf lay a single white flower beside it.

"For Plum," Leaf said.

# CHAPTER SEVENTEEN

LEAF SAT IN THE crook of the tree, staring up at the stars, thinking about Aunt Plum.

She had been so brave. So faithful. She had believed in the Dragon, and in Leaf as the Dragon Speaker. She'd set out to look for answers when no other panda would. And it sounded like she'd stood up to Dusk, until the very end. . . .

What would Aunt Plum say about the Dragon Speaker's stone?

*She would have something to say,* Leaf thought. *She might even know what to do.*

It hurt that Rain hadn't told her, even though Leaf understood why. It was almost worse that the Hollowtree pandas hadn't either—several of them had known, and they'd simply assumed she did too. It wasn't their fault, but it still hurt.

Would she have acted differently when they were

confronting Dusk, if she'd known what he'd done?

Maybe not.

*You'd be proud of us, Aunt Plum,* she thought. *If you could see how the pandas all came around . . . you'd be so proud.*

"Leaf? Are you up there?"

Leaf sniffed and cleared her throat as Rain's head appeared through the canopy. "Yes, I'm here."

"Can I come up?"

Leaf nodded, and then watched as her sister clambered up the tree, her paws slipping a little. Leaf wasn't sure whether to interrupt—Rain was missing the obvious paw holds, and overreaching when she tried to swap branches, making everything harder for herself. Finally Rain threw out her paws, grabbed the branch Leaf was sitting on, and then found she was stretched too far to either get up or let go. She had to hop, which made both branches sway dangerously, and Leaf finally leaned down and grabbed her scruff in her jaws to help her up.

Rain clung to the branch for a moment; then she finally relaxed and sat next to Leaf.

She didn't say anything for a while. Leaf saw her turn her face to the moon and sigh.

"I wish Plum and Peony had had a chance to talk," Leaf said at last. "They both knew Orchid. I think they would have liked to talk about her."

Rain gave Leaf a slightly desperate look, as if she wanted to apologize again but knew that saying sorry wouldn't make it any better.

Leaf stared up at the stars again and thought she saw one of them wink at her . . . and then another, and then another! For a moment she stared into the sky, not understanding what was happening, and then she heard the squeaking and the rustling sound of small wings.

"Hold on," she told Rain, and Rain managed to dig her claws into the tree trunk just as the bats reached the tree. They zipped all around the two pandas, never hitting them or the branches or even the leaves, but darting through the smallest gaps and all around their heads, until one by one they landed. The tiny mouselike creatures, with their strange little noses and leathery wings, hung from branches all around Leaf and Rain.

"Friends!" Leaf said, hope surging in her heart. "Do you have any news of our triplet?"

"Any trace at all?" Rain asked. "Male or female? North or south?"

The bats all spoke at once, but through the cacophony Leaf could make out their meaning.

"Not in the north, not in the south," came the squeaked reply. "Not at all in the forests."

Leaf tried not to slump too heavily against the tree trunk as her hopes ebbed away again. Rain let a long breath out and threw her head back in annoyance.

"Thank you," she managed to say. "Thank you for trying."

The bats squeaked again, and Leaf thought she sensed their disappointment alongside Rain's and her own. They took off once more, and circled around the tree before melting into the night.

After they were gone, Leaf threw her paws up and slumped back.

"I don't know what we do now," she said.

Rain picked at a bit of moss on the tree trunk with one claw. "Not give up," she said. "For a start."

"I'm not," Leaf retorted, sharply enough that Rain looked up in surprise. Leaf took a deep breath, and felt her face crumple a little. "I—I just wish Plum were here," she said. "I miss her, and—and I'm so worried about Dasher! What if he's out there hurt somewhere, just like Plum was? What if I never know about it until it's too late?"

"Hey," Rain said, shifting closer to Leaf. Leaf leaned against her shoulder and let Rain give her a small, encouraging lick on the ear. "That little creature's much tougher than he looks. Remember him and Shadowhunter? I thought Dasher was going to try to fight a tiger the whole time we were on that mountain together."

"Dash has been through a lot," Leaf agreed. "We walked so far looking for our triplet, and then looking for you. We ran into monkeys and wild boars—and he knew Pepper was lying long before I did."

"Yeah, see?" Rain said. "He'll be—"

Leaf turned to look at Rain. Her sister's mouth was open, her eyes fixed on something on the ground, at the base of the tree. Leaf followed her gaze. There was someone down there—a panda shape, sitting at the bottom of the tree, looking up at them. For a moment Leaf couldn't see the panda's face, as if it were a shadow in the shape of a panda. Then, like the moon coming out from behind a cloud, light filled the shape, and Leaf almost fell out of the tree.

"Plum!" she gasped. She slid from the branch to the one below, leaning over as far as she could, but the bear below them was, unmistakably, Plum Slenderwood.

"It can't be," Rain said, scrambling down after her.

"But it is! Plum!" Leaf called. "Wait there—don't move — I'm coming down!"

She half climbed, half fell out of the tree, ignoring a splinter that jabbed into her back paw, letting herself slide down the trunk by her claws, thudding onto the ground on her haunches and falling over and then leaping back to her paws. She heard Rain grunting and cursing her clumsy paws as she tried to climb down after her, and then a thump and another curse as she landed in a pile of leaves. But Leaf couldn't take her eyes off Plum.

She was really here, but . . .

"Plum, it's me!" she called out, and bounded toward her. But Plum didn't reply. She looked at Leaf with a soft expression, and then turned and walked away. "Rain, you can see her, right?"

"Yes!" Rain panted, staggering to Leaf's side. "She looks . . . oh . . ."

Leaf's heart ached as she watched Plum move through the

trees. There was something strange about her—that sense of a shadow passed over her and then melted away again, but all around her the moonlight was bright and there were no clouds in the sky.

"Come on," Rain said. "We've got to go after her."

"Right," said Leaf, and sprang into a run. She hopped over tree roots and scattered leaves as she went, trying to catch up to the shadowy figure of Plum—but no matter how she pushed herself, she never seemed to get any closer. Plum always remained a few bear-lengths ahead, walking at a measured pace. Sometimes she even stopped to look back at Leaf and at Rain, and blink softly or nod, but Leaf couldn't get close to her even when she did.

"This is . . . what is this?" Rain panted, after a burst of speed. "A vision? Is it really her?"

Leaf couldn't answer.

They followed Plum across a stream, around the trunk of a towering tree as wide as the Hollow Fir, and up and over a pile of mossy rocks, until all of a sudden Leaf burst out from the shadow of the trees and found herself on a steep hill of craggy rock, under bright silver moonlight.

Plum was standing on the hill, already many bear-lengths ahead. Out in the open, she seemed to shine as she looked down on Leaf: bright silver where her fur had once been white, and as black as the deep night sky where her markings had been. The scar on her face from the white monster looked like a seam of silver running through rock.

She smiled again. Then she turned and headed up the hill, and now Leaf could see that she was moving nothing at all like she had the last time Leaf had seen her—she climbed over the rocks like a young panda, full of energy.

Leaf headed up after her, with Rain scrambling behind. She knew now that she would never be able to catch Plum—only follow her to wherever they were heading. The hill was steeper and higher than it had looked at first, and she stopped several times to check that Rain was climbing the rocks all right, but Rain seemed to be having a better time with rocks than trees—or perhaps her curiosity to see what Plum was leading them to was giving her extra strength.

Panting, Leaf pushed up and up, until finally there was just one final ledge to climb. She paused to help Rain up over it, and looked back, her head spinning with the effort. They were so high up now, she could see every other hill in the Northern Forest below them. The Hollowtree clearing was a deep valley, and the Darkpool was somewhere on the other side of a farther hill, and beyond them, though she couldn't quite make it out, she knew there was the river.

Together, Rain and Leaf clambered up over the ledge.

There, on the other side, Leaf saw a wide, stony ridge bathed in the silver moonlight, the top snaking its way toward the White Spine Mountains. The light was so bright that she could see the clouds moving across the peaks. She almost felt she could see a snowstorm, swirling over the wide white slopes.

Plum was standing there, facing them, waiting. Leaf took a

few wobbly steps toward her, and this time Plum didn't move.

But out from behind her, seeming out of the thin air, stepped another creature.

It was a snow leopard—like Shiver, but much bigger, moving gracefully as she padded across the stones and sat up straight beside Plum, her huge tail curled neatly around her paws.

*And I thought Shiver was pretty large,* Leaf thought.

But she had none of the fear she had originally held for Shadowhunter, even though there was no mistaking the eyes of a hunter.

"What in the name of the Dragon . . . ?" Rain muttered, stumbling to a breathless halt beside Leaf.

And there was another figure too—a second panda, an adult female who stood on the other side of Plum, her white fur shining. She touched her nose to Plum's, and as the two pandas smiled at each other, a sense of peace washed over Leaf for the first time since she'd heard of Plum's death.

This new panda looked a lot like Plum, Leaf thought. And her eyes, the way she tilted her head as she turned back to look at them . . . she reminded Leaf of Rain. . . .

"Oh," Leaf gasped. "Rain, it's . . . I think . . . no, I know. It's Orchid!"

"It's our mother," Rain said, in a choked voice. She stepped forward a little, her eyes shining.

All three of them, Orchid and Plum and the strange white leopard, turned to look behind them. Leaf followed their gaze and saw, beyond the snowstorm and the drifting clouds, the

Dragon Mountain in the distance. Leaf wasn't sure if she was really seeing it, or if it was another part of the vision—it seemed to glow faintly.

As she watched, the leopard turned and walked along the ridge. She went to the crest of the hill, looked back at them with a knowing smile, and then walked over it and disappeared.

Leaf knew what would happen next, but she didn't want it to. As Plum turned to follow the leopard, she wanted to cry out to her to stop, to please just stay a little longer. But she couldn't find the strength to break the powerful silence that had fallen over all of them. Plum gave her a last nod, full of resolve, and then she went over the hill and vanished too.

Orchid turned to go as well, and she too looked back before she disappeared. It was a moment that Leaf wished could last forever. Their mother looked down at both of them, love and pride written softly across her face. She didn't need to speak. Leaf knew.

Then Orchid winked. Rain let out a shocked laugh, and Leaf sat down heavily on her haunches, her breath shallow.

And then Orchid was gone.

Leaf seemed to suddenly find the strength to move again, and she rushed to the crest of the hill and looked down, but—of course—there was nothing there. Only the winding ridge leading to the White Spine, and the Dragon Mountain shining in the distance.

The moonlight was still bright, but the night seemed twice

as dark without the three visions standing in front of them. Leaf sank down onto her belly and let out a thin whine.

"What is this?" she asked. "Why would the Dragon show us our mother—why would it bring Plum back to me, only to take her away again? And—and who was the *leopard*? Is it something to do with Shiver? I don't understand!" Leaf wailed.

There was a long silence. Leaf looked over at Rain and saw that she was staring into the mountains as if seeing another vision—but there was nothing there.

"No. I don't believe it," Rain muttered.

"What?"

"I . . ." Rain kept staring ahead for another few moments, and then a tiny smile creased the corners of her muzzle and she looked away. "No, it's probably nothing. I just can't believe we got to see Orchid. And I think I know what we need to do," she added, pointing with her nose toward the mountains.

"But that doesn't make any sense," Leaf said. "Last time we went to the Dragon Mountain, we couldn't get near it because we hadn't found the third triplet. Why wouldn't that happen again?"

"Well . . . if the Great Dragon thinks this time we should go, then that's what we have to do, right? I mean, Leaf . . . it sent our mothers to tell us what to do!" She chuckled to herself again. "Apart from Peony, I mean. I think we have to listen to them."

Leaf got to her paws. "You're right. Of course! Plum wouldn't steer me wrong. The Dragon sent her to show us the way to the mountains—why would we do anything else?" She shook herself from head to toe. "What happened to me being the one who believed, and you doubting everything?"

Rain walked over and nuzzled the side of Leaf's head. "I think we met in the middle," she said.

They returned to the Hollowtree clearing just as the Feast of Moon Fall was underway. They ate, surrounded by the largest gathering of pandas Leaf had ever seen. She could hardly believe it when Rain said that this wasn't even all the Prosperhill pandas. They decided to get some sleep before they set out, so they climbed up into the low branches of a tree, and the next thing Leaf knew she was waking up as dawn poured over the clearing and the pandas and red pandas stirred for the Feast of Gray Light.

They waited until the feast was done, and then Leaf stood and told the assembled pandas and red pandas their plans.

"We've had a vision from the Great Dragon," she said, but she didn't tell them what it had been. She wasn't sure why, but for now she wanted to keep Plum's and Orchid's appearance to herself. Later she was sure she'd share it with the others.

The Hollowtree pandas were concerned but supportive. Seeker Climbing Far came over to her, and she repeated Rain's reassurances about Dasher, but in her heart she was still worried.

"I wish he were here. It feels wrong to set out on an adventure without Dasher," she told Seeker.

"Why don't I go out and look for him?" said a voice, and Leaf turned to see Shiver sitting nearby. "He's seen me before, so he won't be afraid," she added, glancing at some of the other red pandas, who were giving the leopard a very, very wide berth. "I want to search for Ghost, too," she said softly. "I know he hasn't deliberately abandoned us."

"Thank you," Leaf said. "That would be very kind of you." She paused, looking over at Rain. Should she mention the white leopard in their vision? It *must* be something to do with Shiver, mustn't it?

Rain stepped up to the snow leopard. "Hey, Shiver, can I have a word . . . over there?" she asked, nodding at the shadow of a large gingko where there was nobody else standing.

"Okay . . . ," Shiver said cautiously, and followed Rain over.

Other pandas began coming up to Leaf and giving her their best wishes and advice for the journey, so she was a little distracted, but she did look over every few moments to see Rain and Shiver talking in the shade of the gingko. Though she couldn't hear their conversation, she did see Shiver sit down heavily on her haunches, and then she saw her tail start to curl in excitement, and heard her give a chirruping laugh.

They said their final goodbyes, took hold of a jawful of bamboo each, at Grass's insistence, for the Feast of Sun Climb, and then set off through the forest, heading once more for the long rocky hill and the ridge that would lead them toward the mountains.

"Can we just eat this?" Rain said, putting down her bamboo

as soon as they'd gone far enough from the Hollow Fir that they wouldn't be overheard by a wandering panda. "I know it's not time for the feast, but I don't want to carry it up those rocks!"

"Good idea," said Leaf, and they settled down and made quick work of the bamboo canes. Leaf tried to savor every last delicious bite. She remembered their last trip to the mountain, and she expected to be eating insects again before this was over.

"Did Shiver know who the leopard was we saw?" Leaf asked eagerly, as soon as she'd finished her bamboo cane.

"She thought it was her mother," Rain said. "She died in the mountains, before Shiver left."

"Oh! But why would her mother have come to help us?"

But before Rain could answer, Leaf heard a cracking noise in the undergrowth nearby, and looked up. Was it one of the pandas following them for some reason? Could it be Dasher, come to join them?

Whatever it was, it stopped moving when she stood up. That put her on edge. If something was nearby that didn't want to be seen . . .

"Come on," she told Rain. Her sister was already on her paws and backing away.

The steep rock hill was still a tough climb in the daylight, but Leaf was glad that they'd moved out of the shadow of the trees. If anything wanted to creep up on them, it would have a much more difficult job.

The mountains definitely looked farther away in the daylight, and the Dragon Mountain wasn't visible at all behind a bank of gray cloud. But they knew it was the right way to go now, so they started to walk the long, winding ridge that led toward the foothills of the White Spine.

They walked all day, missing the feasts of High Sun and Long Light altogether, but stopping for Sun Fall when they spotted a stand of bamboo growing out of the side of the hill just below the ridge. Leaf climbed down and fetched the canes up onto the flat, stony path, and they ate them watching the bright sun vanish behind the trees on the next hill.

A chill enveloped them as they walked on, through Dying Light and Moon Climb, until finally Leaf found that her paws were aching. They found a tree, a twisted pine that grew sideways out of the side of the hill, and climbed the trunk to curl up in the wide crook between its branches.

Leaf woke with a gasp, to discover that it was still dark, probably not yet Moon Fall. Something had woken her . . . something that was poking at her paw, insistently.

Leaf scrambled to her paws, half-awake and afraid, and raised her claws to swipe at whatever it was, predator or scavenger. . . .

But the pale shape crouching on the tree trunk in front of her was whispering her name.

"Leaf? Leaf, don't! It's me!"

She blinked, and then shook her head, trying to make sure she was really seeing what her eyes told her she was seeing.

It was *Pepper.*

"Pepper, what in the name of the Dragon are you doing here?" Leaf said, sitting down again and pawing at her eyes, trying to clear them. "We're so far from home! Did you follow us all day?"

"Shhh!" Pepper said. "You've got to be quiet!"

"Wha—?" Rain groaned, sitting up beside them. "Who's . . . is that Pepper? What are you doing here? You're *not* a Dragon Speaker, you know," she added, a little more harshly than Leaf would have. "You can't come to the mountain with us. Go home to your mother!"

"It's not that!" Pepper hissed. "I'm here to warn you! No stories this time! I saw him following you, so I followed him, and when he stopped for the feast I ran around him and got in front so I could warn you. Dusk is here!"

# CHAPTER EIGHTEEN

"Are you *sure* you can trust this cub?" Rain panted. She tried to whisper to Leaf, but she didn't really care that much if Pepper heard her. Her paws were getting sore from running across the loose stones on the ridge in the darkness, and if she found out that all this was for nothing . . .

"What would you rather do?" Leaf hissed back. "Ignore him and wait for Dusk to find us?"

"Good point," Rain said, and put on an extra burst of speed.

She was sure that Dusk had no intention of quietly vanishing. *The way he looked at me . . . And he's inventive; he proved that with the pit. If it's him and his thugs against us two—well, three—we have to shake him off, or we'll never make it to the Dragon Mountain.*

"Come on," Pepper told them. "There's a good place to hide nearby, this way. It's *real*," he added, seeing the look Rain was giving him. "I came up here when I got separated from Mother. I thought I'd be able to see her if I was high up."

"That sounds about right," said Leaf softly. Rain guessed she could see what Leaf meant—the idea was slightly delusional, so it did sound like something Pepper might have thought of.

"If you trust him, I trust him," she said, trying to shrug without slowing down.

All day, both sides of the ridge had sloped down into forest valleys, but now on the left the land had risen to meet it. Pepper led them that way, into a thin pine forest where there was almost no undergrowth but rocks and crunching pine needles. They began to fight their way uphill, weaving between tree trunks. Rain looked behind them, but in the dark she couldn't see much farther than a few bear-lengths back.

And then she spotted it—a flash of white fur, somewhere to their left. Then another, farther ahead. She heard paws on the pine needles that weren't hers or Leaf's or Pepper's. She almost ran into a tree as she tried to focus on the moving white shapes, and finally caught a full look at them as they pounded alongside the running Dragon Speakers.

"He's right—it's them!" she hissed to Leaf. "Dusk, and he's still got Blossom and Ginseng with him!"

"Oh, Dragon," Leaf groaned.

"Pepper, this hiding place . . . ," Rain prompted him.

"Just a bit farther!"

"Pepper," Rain said more urgently. Up ahead, was that a

panda shape lurking half-concealed behind a tree?

Dusk and his thugs were bigger and stronger. They could have pulled ahead. They could be waiting to ambush them. . . .

"All right, follow me!" Pepper said, and took an abrupt right turn. Rain skidded to follow him, kicking up needles.

All of a sudden, the pine forest was full of bamboo, the spaces between trees no longer wide spaces but crowded with huge bamboo canes, as broad as Rain's shoulders. It was a thicket so large and dense that Rain couldn't see the edge of it.

"Go on!" Pepper said. "Go through there, right into the middle!"

Leaf took a deep breath and squeezed through a small gap between canes, bending them aside, and Rain scrambled after her. She had to claw the ground and wiggle to get her hind-quarters through, but she made it, and found herself in a thick maze of green, wavering bamboo.

"There's a way through," Leaf said, nosing at a gap where two stands had almost but not entirely merged together. She looked around. "Where's Pepper?"

He hadn't come through with them. Rain pressed her eye to the gap between canes and caught her breath.

Pepper was a few bear-lengths in front of the canes, sitting close to the trunk of a tall pine tree. And out of the shadow of the trees, Dusk, Blossom, and Ginseng were prowling, their heads held low and menacing.

Leaf crept to Rain's side and peered through the gaps between the canes. She took a horrified breath that Rain briefly thought might give them away—but Dusk was focused completely on the cub sitting in the pine needles in front of him.

"You lied to me, Pepper," Dusk growled. "And Ghost lied when he told me he'd killed you. Now you will tell me the truth. Where are your sisters?"

Rain's eyes went wide. *He still thinks Pepper's one of us.* Her stomach cramped with worry. Pepper looked tiny beside the hulking forms of Dusk and his thugs. *They'll tear him to bits. . . .*

"We'll find them," Blossom growled. "Whether you tell us or not."

"Don't hurt me," Pepper whined. "They doubled back! Back to the ridge!"

"So they left you here all alone," Dusk sneered. His lips drew back to show Pepper his teeth. "And now I'm going to kill you."

Rain tensed. If she sprang from the bamboo as he lunged for Pepper, she would be able to get a swipe across Dusk's nose, and—

Pepper leaped at the tree trunk, and Rain realized there was a low branch too thin for a full-sized panda to climb on, but perfect for a cub like Pepper. He scrambled onto it as if he were part squirrel, before any of the other pandas could react.

"Catch me first!" he crowed, and then he was gone, up onto a higher branch, running along it and into the next tree, a spindly thing that bent under his weight but didn't break.

"After him!" Dusk roared. He and Blossom ran along

the ground, snarling up at the escaping Pepper. Ginseng attempted to climb the tree, and Rain held her breath . . . and sure enough, he tried to put a paw on the thin branch and it snapped under him, sending him sprawling onto the ground. He got up and snorted, and then ran off after the other two.

Pepper, meanwhile, had made a scrambling hop for the next canopy, and vanished from Rain's line of sight.

Rain pulled back. She listened hard for anything that might be a fateful snap of a branch or the triumphant cry of an adult panda, but all she heard was Dusk's far-too-familiar angry bellowing, and the rustle of paws in pine needles, growing farther and farther away.

She met Leaf's eyes, and they stared at each other for a long moment.

"He saved us," Leaf whispered. She closed her eyes. "Oh, Dragon, please protect him, please let him get back home safely. . . ."

"You were right to trust him," Rain said.

"It's not just that. I didn't know before why the Dragon would have had the bats lead me to him, if he was only going to lie to me and lead me off course. But following him brought me to the Hollow Fir, which brought him to his mother, and me to you, and us to this moment. . . . None of this would have happened if it hadn't been for Pepper!"

"Let's get out of here," Rain said, feeling like her brain was expanding a little too far. She pushed her way into the gap between the bamboo stands, and they made their way through the maze of canes until they found that it ended at another steep, rocky slope. It wasn't too sheer or too high to climb, so they paused just long enough to eat some of the leaves from the bamboo—afraid to chomp down the canes themselves in case the sound of the snap traveled.

Then they clambered up and out of the bamboo forest, hanging on to scrub and lifting themselves over more of the horizontal pines, with their roots dug deep into the rock, trunks that could be walked along and branches that stuck out or straight up into the air. Rain paused, sitting on the trunk of a high-up pine tree, to look back down at the bamboo and the forest they had left behind. The sun was coming up, illuminating the dark green canopy, and there was no sign of Dusk, or of Pepper.

There was no end to the climbing. Either they were pulling themselves over rocks, paw over paw, or they were resting in the tops of trees, or they were walking up slopes. There was less and less cover, and more and more chill in the air.

Another High Sun came and went, and with the bamboo forest far behind them, they made their first feast of worms and beetles from underneath a rock—a stage on their journey that Rain thought she and Leaf had both been prepared for, but really weren't looking forward to.

By the time the sun set on the second day of walking, Rain was exhausted, and extremely happy to wriggle into a small cave in the side of a rock that smelled like it had once been home to rabbits or maybe pikas, and sleep as if the fate of the kingdom depended on it. But when they got up, just before dawn, she found she was rested and surprisingly full of energy. Maybe those beetles had been more filling than she'd thought.

They talked more, on the third day of walking. It was partly to distract themselves from the chill that started to get under their fur, but they didn't talk about that. They talked about what had happened to them both since they split up, sharing almost every detail.

Leaf told Rain how scared she'd been when she'd found her family poisoned by the water in the pool, how she'd tried not to let herself think about it, but she'd known in her heart that little Cane and his mother, Hyacinth, could easily have died. Rain shuddered, and told Leaf all about her attempts to confront Dusk, how infuriating and terrifying it had been when Pebble, and all the other pandas she had grown up with, turned against her. She'd trusted them with her life, even when they didn't get along. Even Ginseng had always been kind, in an aloof sort of way.

"Apart from Blossom," she added. "I always hated Blossom—she's the worst."

At Long Light, they came across some goji bushes laden with berries, and ate every single one, even the ones that weren't truly ripe yet. Rain thought about Pepper's mother, and said another quiet prayer to the Dragon that he had made it back to her.

The worst part of the whole journey, Rain thought later,

was that afternoon, which they spent clambering over rocks covered in frost. They were slippery, and her paws stung with cold. It was a relief when the first snowbanks began to appear, piled up against the rocky crags and in the shadows of trees. Before dark they were walking in thick, white snow that crunched under their paws. It wasn't exactly like treading on grass—Rain slipped and fell face first into it twice—but at least it was a soft landing.

They walked on, up through the White Spine Mountains, picking their way through deep snow and pushing through storms that swept ice and thick white flakes into their faces, arriving and passing again as fast as the wind would take them. Sun Fall, Dying Light, and Moon Climb went by, until they were traveling under the light of the stars. Neither of them wanted to stop just yet—as long as it wasn't actually snowing on them, they had to keep on going.

Rain suddenly thought she recognized something—a particular cliff face, the way that the ledge they were on wound around it. Was this the same way they'd come the first time, to get to the long canyon that led through the mountains to the far peak of the Dragon Mountain? It was dark, though, and she told herself not to get too excited. She could be imagining it. All the cliffs and rocks and snow looked close to identical to her. It was still probably a long way off, and even if they did get to the canyon, they would still have that wall of rock that had blocked their path before to contend with.

But after they'd gone a little farther, scrambling up a steep snowbank to stand on the edge of a wide white shelf, Leaf stopped walking. Rain saw the breath making clouds in front of her face as she looked around. The snow was starting to fall again now, drifting around them in the soft, lovely way that made Rain suspicious that a real ice storm was probably right behind it.

"That peak looks so familiar," Leaf said, nosing through the snow toward the edge of the shelf, where the mountain rose up into a craggy spire, and the snow around it showed a path of rocks that they could climb to circle around it.

Rain led the way. She wasn't sure if she was shivering more from the cold or from the anticipation. She'd recognized this peak too. She followed the path, treading carefully, sleet blowing into her eyes, until she could look down the other side.

And there it was, as clear as it had been when they'd last come this far: the path down the side of the mountain and into the chasm, which cut through forests' worth of jagged rocks and sheer cliff edges, all the way to the Dragon Mountain.

The snow stopped as Leaf clambered around the edge of the peak. The clouds parted and blew away, and the mountain itself came into view, dark against the stars, but so close.

Then the clouds came back. Flurries of snow seemed to chase the two pandas as they made their way to the opening of the chasm. They walked into it, and soon they saw ahead the same pile of rocks that had blocked their path. Rain shuddered as she looked at them, remembering the sight of Leaf falling from the very top, rocks rolling down after her, almost crushing her.

She realized just how cold and tired she felt, and she looked at Leaf.

"You only just made it before," she said, "when they were freshly fallen, and you weren't so tired, and it was daytime and not snowing. Let's find somewhere to sleep. In the morning we might be able to find another way around them."

Rain was a little bit afraid that Leaf might refuse and insist on trying to climb the rocks right now. But she turned to Rain and nodded, exhaustion making her ears droop.

"Look," Leaf said. "There's an overhang there that's a bit out of the wind and the snow."

They hurried over and squeezed themselves up against the rock wall. It was more sheltered than the open air, at least. Thoughts of earthquakes and falling rocks rose in Rain's mind, but she squashed them as she stamped down the snow to make a space for them to curl up in. She was cold and tired right through to her bones. And after all, there was a good chance they'd freeze to death before an earthquake had time to crush them.

She didn't share any of these thoughts with Leaf. She didn't have time—Leaf had already settled down, pressed her nose to Rain's side, and fallen asleep. Rain tucked her own nose in under her paws, and in a moment she was gone.

She woke up to an earthquake.

The shaking ground and the roar that echoed down the

chasm brought Rain from unconsciousness to a run in one panicked movement. She shot out from under the overhang into the intense orange glare of the sunrise, skidded in the snow, and turned back to call for Leaf, only to find that her sister had woken too and was right behind her. They came to a shaky stop, clinging to each other and looking around at the chasm walls.

Then Rain noticed something over Leaf's shoulder.

"Leaf," she shouted over the noise. "Look!"

The previous rockfall was crumbling away. The stones at its base were being shaken loose. As they watched, boulders rolled from the top and struck the ground, and others crumbled, falling into dust and blowing away. A space opened up in the center of the rock pile, and a cascade of fresh snow was shaken off the cliffs, falling into the gap, forming something that looked eerily like a clear, white path across the rocks.

The tremors stopped, and the mountains fell silent.

"Leaf," Rain whispered. "I think maybe we're supposed to be here this time."

"Come on," Leaf said in a small voice. "Let's go to the Dragon Mountain."

They continued up to the path and started to climb the gentle slope. Rain led the way, still walking extremely carefully, examining the ground with every step. She passed through the open gap, and looked down the slope on the other side to see the chasm, the Dragon Mountain glowing fiery in the sunrise, and . . .

There was a creature standing in the middle of the chasm, right in front of them, staring up at the crumbled rock wall and then down at Rain with total astonishment on his face.

Rain felt a wide smile growing on her face. It was Ghost.

She forgot about the danger of the rocks and ran toward him, her paws kicking up snow.

"It is you!" she laughed. "It is, I knew it!"

"Rain, what's happening?" Leaf called, chasing after her. "Who is this? Is . . . is this . . ."

Rain stopped just short of running right into Ghost. He leaned back a little, and she couldn't blame him—she hadn't exactly been this keen to see him last time they'd met. But things were different now.

"Leaf, this is Ghost," she said. "He lived in the Southern Forest for a while. He's a panda—I know he looks different, but he is. He's an orphan . . . he was *raised by leopards.*"

Leaf's eyes went wide.

"I thought it could be," Rain went on, babbling a little in her excitement, "I mean, it kind of had to be, but I didn't want to say anything, because what if I was wrong, and anyway I knew I didn't know where he was, and—hey, Ghost, raise your paw for me," Rain said.

"What are you going on about?" Ghost demanded.

"Come on," Rain said, patting the snow in front of her. "I bet you've been through some pretty weird stuff to get here. Just put your paw up."

Ghost sighed and raised his paw. His grip pad was white.

Of course it was—all his pads were white. And not the pale pinkish color that some pandas had instead of black or brown; they were *white*. Just like Rain's and Leaf's grip pads were.

Rain raised her own paw, and Leaf did the same. "We're like him, just a little bit—just enough that we'd know! Makes sense now, right?"

Leaf nodded slowly.

"No!" Ghost said. "Nothing has really made sense in quite a long time. And if you don't tell me what in the Snow Cat's name you're talking about, I'm going to take this and leave." And he put his muzzle down into the snow. Rain saw him moving his tongue to take something from inside his cheek, and then . . .

Leaf gasped, but Rain just stared as a shimmering blue stone dropped into the snow.

"All right. That answers *that* question, then." Leaf giggled. "Let me try to start from the beginning. . . . I'm Leaf," she said to Ghost. "And I'm your sister. And so is Rain. And we're Dragon Speakers, all three of us."

For a second, Ghost looked like he was going to tell her she was lying, but then Rain saw the expression on his face change. She knew exactly how he was feeling. Things that had made no sense before were suddenly falling into place. Doubts were melting away.

"We're the triplets," she said. "We're together, at last. And now . . . we're going to see the Dragon."

# CHAPTER NINETEEN

DRAGON SPEAKER. DRAGON *Speakers!*

Ghost kept turning the words over in his mind as he walked along the bottom of the chasm toward the Dragon Mountain, beside his sisters.

*Sisters!*

He was holding the blue stone in his cheek, the Dragon Speaker's stone.

*Our stone!*

Every other thought that passed through his head, he found he had to stop and examine it in a new light.

Could he really speak to the Great Dragon? Well, he had seen the footprints of the Snow Cat. Winter had said the Snow Cat had sent him to her. Perhaps it really had been keeping him safe, so he could be here to do . . . whatever came next.

The new one, Leaf, hadn't been too clear. She'd only said that her aunt—*their aunt*—had said there was a ritual, or something. That only Dragon Speakers knew exactly what it was.

The floor of the chasm had started to gently slope upward, the rock walls growing shallower. The Dragon Mountain loomed ahead of them, the distinctive clouds swirling around its peak.

"So, Sunset—the real one—he used the stone to speak directly to the Dragon?"

"I . . . think so," said Leaf. "I'm not really sure."

"Does that mean only one of us will be able to speak to it at once?" Rain asked.

Ghost hadn't thought of that. From the silence that followed, he suspected Leaf hadn't either.

"You didn't seem very surprised that Dusk wasn't really Sunset," Leaf said, and Ghost wondered if she was changing the subject. "Did you know, somehow?"

"Not specifically, no," Ghost said quickly. "I didn't know he'd killed someone and taken his place. I just . . . I've seen his rage, and I know he's a liar. He'd say anything, and hurt anyone, if it got him what he wanted."

Ghost stopped briefly and looked back as they emerged from the chasm. He was shocked to find himself looking down on the White Spine Mountains. Somewhere below him was Winter's den, his leopard siblings, the Endless Maw, everything he had ever known. Possibly everything that existed, apart from the mountain they were standing on.

It had looked purple from a distance, except for the blazing orange where the sun would hit it at sunrise and sunset. Close up, the rising, jagged rocks were so dark they were almost black. The mountain seemed to spring out of the earth, as suddenly as a mountain possibly could—it looked almost as if the whole peak had been forced up from the ground a little at a time.

"Can you smell that?" Rain said suddenly. Ghost saw her peering up into the sky, and followed her gaze.

The clouds that always seemed to encircle the peak of the Dragon Mountain like smoke . . . they *were* smoke, visible even through the drifting snow. The closer they walked to the jutting rocks, the grayer the flakes falling around them became—whether they were ash or smoke-tinged snow, Ghost couldn't tell. He walked up to the stone of the mountain and put one paw on the black rock.

There was a great roar, like the sound of an earthquake. The rock trembled under his paw, but when he reared back and fell into the snow, the ground wasn't shaking. The roaring went on and on, and then it faded.

"Is that the Dragon?" Leaf asked, her voice wavering with fear and excitement.

"If it is, it's . . . big," said Rain.

"*Big?*" Ghost gasped at her understatement. "I think *unimaginably huge* might be closer to the truth!"

"Well, we have to find a way up, right?" Leaf said. "I don't think we're supposed to stand around here staring at it."

"Who knows?" Rain said in a slightly strangled voice. "Maybe we've done it. We brought the stone, we're Dragon Speakers . . . we can go home now."

Ghost and Leaf both gave her skeptical looks.

"All right," she said. "Maybe not."

It didn't take them long to find the way. Just as the black rocks had burst out of the earth, leaving Ghost with no doubt whatsoever that they had come to the peak, when he spotted the path it was clear which way they had to go. He pointed it out to the others: a rock ledge, about the width of two pandas, but not wide enough for them to walk side by side. It was thick with snow, so it looked like a white snake curling up around the mountain.

"Or a dragon," Leaf pointed out.

"There's barely room to squeeze past each other," Ghost pointed out, as he sniffed at the ledge where it rose out of the ground at the base of the peak. "So I guess we have to go single file."

"Which means someone has to go first," said Leaf.

Rain sighed. "I'll do it," she said. "I just don't want to stand here and talk about it."

She stepped onto the ledge, and Ghost saw her feeling for her balance—it wasn't *that* small a ledge, but he guessed he couldn't blame her. It sloped upward pretty steeply, and within a few bear-lengths she would be a dangerous distance from the ground if she slipped off the edge.

Leaf went next, and Ghost brought up the rear, careful

of where he put his paws, his sisters' prints making the snow more stable, but more slippery, too.

They wound their way around the mountain, moving slowly, stopping for breath often.

"It's okay," Ghost called forward, remembering suddenly that neither of the others had spent much time in snow, apart from the climb to get here. "Try to keep your weight even, but don't obsess about it; it doesn't help. Keep moving, if you can. If you're taking a break, sit down, spread your weight over a bigger area, so there's less chance of slipping."

"Thanks, Ghost," said Leaf. Rain didn't say anything. "Rain says thanks too," Leaf added.

They walked on, and Ghost kept a close watch on his sisters, hoping that if anything went wrong, he would be able to grab them in time. It helped him keep his mind off his own paws.

After a while, he heard Rain gasp up ahead. Then Leaf leaned in to the rock a little, and a few paw steps later Ghost saw why: On this side of the mountain, there was no soft snowfield below them, or even the ordinary rolling peaks of gray rock; here there was nothing below them but a steep, sheer drop into darkness. Ghost knew that if they fell from this height, even if they fell into the snow at the base of the black rock, they might not survive. But somehow it was still worse when he couldn't even make out where his body might land, and it was a small relief when they'd walked far enough around the peak that the ground came back, even if it was now far below them.

How far did this path go? Would they walk all the way to the top?

Ghost was about to call up and ask Rain if she could see anything, when he heard a small sound, like stones falling. He froze, and then very carefully looked over his shoulder.

There was nothing there. He turned back, but then there it was again: the sound of stones bouncing off the rocks. This time he turned in time to catch it: a few small rocks skittering down the side of the mountain and landing in the snow on the path behind him. He looked up.

Dusk was staring down at him, eyes wide and furious and triumphant. He was standing with Blossom and Ginseng, on the section of path that passed right over the triplets' heads.

"Look out!" Ghost yelled, but it was too late. The three adult pandas slid down the hard black rock and landed on the path, Blossom ahead of Rain, Ginseng in front of Leaf, and Dusk right ahead of Ghost.

Everything happened so fast. Blossom roared and raised her paw to claw at Rain, but Rain roared back and charged her, head-butting her right in the chest before she could even swing. Blossom slipped and fell back on the path, one leg dangling dangerously off the ledge. Ginseng made a bite for Leaf, and managed to get his paws around her, tackling her against the rock of the mountain. But Leaf twisted and got her claws into the rock, and then, using paw holds that Ghost couldn't even see, she hauled herself upward, over the jagged edge of one of the splinters of black rock, where Ginseng couldn't reach her.

And Dusk simply stared at Ghost while the chaos unfolded on the thin path behind him. His eyes were red and hazy, as if he hadn't slept in days.

Ghost felt fury rise inside himself, like the smoke rising from the Dragon Mountain, as he looked into the face of the panda who'd tried to make him into a killer, who'd made him feel valued while stripping away everything that made him who he really was. The manipulation, the lies, the rage when things didn't go his way—all of it condensed into the shape of the animal in front of him.

"Oh, Ghost," said Dusk, shaking his head in mock pity. "It was you all along, and you didn't even know. But do you really think the other pandas will accept a freak like you as a Dragon Speaker?"

"Rain and Leaf do," Ghost snarled. "The others will too, once you're not around to poison them against me."

"Still so eager to fit in," Dusk sneered. "So stupid, so worthless except as a blunt instrument—and you couldn't even get that right. You look like a monster, but deep down you're a coward."

"I saw Brawnshanks smack you down with just a word," Ghost retorted, and he could see that he had stung Dusk. "And you say I'm the coward? Unlike you, *Dusk*, I'm a real Dragon Speaker. No need for bargains with monkeys. My sisters know who I am, and my littermates do too, and that's all that matters. I'll always be part panda, part snow leopard—and my snow-leopard mother taught me how to fight!"

He sprang at Dusk, who was caught off guard for one wonderful moment. Ghost managed to get his paws around the bigger panda's neck and bite down hard on his shoulder. He tasted blood.

But Dusk rallied quickly. He roared and shook himself. Ghost was almost thrown off the side of the mountain, and he scrabbled with his back paws and dug his claws into Dusk's flank until he could let go at the right moment, throwing himself back onto the path and knocking his shoulder heavily against the stone. Dusk brought a paw down, claws slicing through the air, and Ghost pushed himself, sliding on the snow, just in time to see Dusk's paws rake across the path. But Dusk seemed to be ready for this, and jumped forward, bringing his weight down on Ghost's front feet, trapping him there. He bit down, trying to catch Ghost's skull in his jaws, and managed to get hold of one ear. Ghost felt it tear and roared with pain.

Dusk reared back, startled, as Ghost's roar seemed to double in volume. The mountain was roaring again.

"That's the Great Dragon!" Rain declared. Blossom was getting to her paws, but now Ghost saw her cast a terrified look up at the mountain. New horror was dawning in Ginseng's eyes too, and he stopped trying to claw his way up to Leaf's perch. "Yes! It really is! And it's angry with you for attacking its Dragon Speakers!"

"It's your last chance," Leaf yelled down. "To give this up, and maybe spare yourself the Dragon's wrath!"

Dusk advanced on Ghost again. "I'm going to—" he began, but then he fell facedown in the snow as Ginseng clambered right over the top of him. Ghost threw himself against the mountain to give the big panda as much room as he could, and Ginseng shot past him and away down the path.

"I've had enough of this," Blossom snarled. She barged straight past Rain and over Dusk's back before he could straighten up, following Ginseng.

Dusk screamed, "Traitors!" and tried to snap at Blossom's ankles as she passed him, but she was gone after Ginseng, and they were both vanishing around the peak.

"Rain, Leaf, go!" Ghost called, over the dying echoes of the Dragon's roar.

"We can't leave you!" Leaf called back, slipping down onto the path to stand beside Rain.

Dusk was getting back to his paws. Blood seeped from his shoulder and stained the snow beneath him, but he stood strong and furious in front of Ghost, his lips slowly peeling back to show his teeth.

"Just go!" Ghost said. "I'll be all right!"

"Come on," Leaf said, and nudged Rain until she moved.

"I should have gotten rid of you a long time ago," Dusk snarled, his gaze fixed on Ghost. "I should have broken your neck. Now I get to fix that mistake."

He lunged. Ghost was ready for him, and sank to his belly so that Dusk's jaws wouldn't find his neck—but then pain burst against Ghost's side, and he knew, much too late, that

Dusk's snapping jaws had been a distraction. Dusk's claws raked his back, tearing and deepening the monkey wounds that had just begun to heal. Ghost moaned and wriggled away. He slashed wildly at Dusk, and was almost surprised to feel his claws catch on the fake Speaker's flank, where the scar still stood out sharp and pink.

Dusk screamed. Still reeling, Ghost saw the bigger panda's shoulder coming toward him, Dusk's whole body flinging itself sideways to crush Ghost against the mountainside. Ghost tried to move, but his paws slipped on the snow, and then he felt himself slammed with muscle and bone, and his head hit the black rock behind him.

Agony flickered around him like the stars burning out of the sky. He couldn't see. Everything was white. He knew he'd fallen into snow, felt it soft and cool under his head. He must have tripped again. He must have been trying to race Frost or Snowstorm, and fallen into a drift. He should get up, dig his own way out, but it seemed so hard. Would Winter pull him out? Surely she would help him.

And then even the snowdrift faded, and everything went dark.

# CHAPTER TWENTY

"DID WE DO THE right thing?" Leaf muttered. She pounded up the path, kicking up snow, no longer worried about slipping.

*If we can just get all the way around to where Dusk was,* she thought, *we can do what they did: drop down from up here. Maybe we can throw him off the edge. . . .*

But though she looked down onto the path below her, she saw no sign of Ghost or of Dusk. Had they gone far enough? Had they gone too far? What was happening? Was that blood she could see trailing through the snow below them? Whose blood was it?

Another roar sounded, and now she was even more certain than ever that it was coming from inside the mountain. It seemed to her that it was calling her, telling them to hurry. She only hoped she was right. . . .

The end of the path came suddenly. Leaf just managed to stop herself before she ran either off the edge or face-first into the mountain rock. The thin path turned into a wide ledge, and instead of the sheer black rock of the mountain, she was standing next to a gigantic cavern entrance, like a roaring mouth opening onto the Bamboo Kingdom.

Rain let out a surprised yell and then thumped into Leaf's back. Leaf yelped and turned to see Rain's paws slipping on the snowy path. She fell on her back, her back legs dangling briefly but horribly over the end of the ledge, before Leaf grabbed her scruff and scrambled back into the cavern.

The roar had faded, but inside the cavern Leaf could hear a rumbling sound all around her, like a roll of faraway thunder that never ended—or the breathing of a creature the size of a mountain. . . .

"This is it," she murmured, looking into the cave. She couldn't see anything much but darkness. "This must be where we're supposed to go."

She knew she should be excited. This was what it had all been leading to: days of traveling the kingdom, searching and questioning, talking to the bats, fighting off Dusk. This was where she was supposed to be.

So why didn't she want to go in? She forced herself to take a few nervous steps into the dark, her paws grateful to be back on cool, flat stone. But all she felt in her heart was a cold fear. What if Ghost didn't make it? What if this was wrong after all?

"What do you think is in there?" she asked Rain, stalling for time.

"Well," said Rain, pressing her shoulder to Leaf's, "whatever it is, we'll face it together. And Ghost will be here soon," she added.

They walked in, side by side, Leaf's paws trembling as she put them down on the black rock floor. The rumble faded, and soon all she could hear was her own labored breathing, and Rain's beside her.

Beyond the cave mouth, the cavern opened up, walls stretching out on both sides, roof curving up and up and up. The space was vast and dark, and it smelled of smoke and ash, but there was no smoke that Leaf could see. In the middle was a huge patch of what appeared to be darker stone. She looked up and saw that high above, at the peak of the cave, there was light. It was just enough, with the light that pierced the darkness from the cave mouth, to let her eyes adjust so that she could see from end to end of the cavern.

She gasped, and froze, her legs trembling, as she understood what the circle in the middle of the floor really was.

"Rain, careful!" she said.

The vast hole took up most of the middle of the cavern. Rain padded cautiously up to the edge. She looked down, and Leaf heard her intake of breath.

"It's . . . I can't see the bottom of it!" Rain whispered. "What *is* it?"

Leaf swallowed and forced herself to move closer. The light

from the peak above barely penetrated a few bear-lengths into the chasm before it was swallowed up by pure, fathomless darkness.

She stepped back hurriedly and sat down on her haunches, looking around at the blank cave walls and then back at the empty pit at the center of it all.

There was *nothing here.*

Rain let out a shaky breath. "Shouldn't the Dragon . . . be in this cave?" she whispered.

"I don't know!" Leaf whispered back.

"Was it . . . stupid of us to think it would be?" Rain said, and Leaf heard panic rising in her voice. It echoed between the high walls of the cavern. "I mean, a real dragon, just living here in the mountain—wouldn't we all *know* if there were any such thing?"

Leaf stood and pressed her trembling nose to Rain's cheek. "There must be *something*," she told her, as firmly as she could. "We were *summoned.*"

"But, but what if . . . ," Rain began, and then she stopped, her eyes wide in the darkness. "Do you hear that?" She spun to face the cave entrance. Leaf looked too, and now she could hear it, the sound of paws crunching on snow. The whiteness outside seemed blinding after peering down into the abyss of the chasm. But a moment later it was broken up by the shape of a panda, silhouetted against the snow, limping a little, but very much alive.

"Ghost!" she cried. "We're in here!"

The panda walked inside the cavern. His shoulders hunched, and he stalked forward. Leaf heard his labored breaths echoing through the cave, deep and rumbling ... and then she saw his black ears, blood dripping from the black fur on his shoulder.

"That's not Ghost." Rain turned to face the oncoming panda, lowering her muzzle and growling.

"So this is the precious Dragon Mountain," Dusk rumbled.

"Where's Ghost?" Leaf demanded, trying to stop herself from shaking. Rain was standing strong and furious beside her. She could do the same, couldn't she?

"Gone," said Dusk simply. "Just as you will be."

Rain roared, and threw herself at him. Dusk was ready for her, and he ducked her first wild claw swipe and came back with one of his own that knocked her to the ground. She let out a high, gasping noise as the air was thrown from her lungs. Dusk left her there, winded, and launched himself over her at Leaf.

Leaf dodged and rolled. She was barely even thinking about escaping Dusk—his teeth caught her back leg, and pain shot all the way up through her spine, but she almost didn't care. All she wanted was to be farther from the edge of the chasm! Dusk let go, rearing back to bite down harder, but Leaf managed to roll over and kick him under the chin with her other leg. She heard his teeth click together, and hoped he'd bitten his tongue. He staggered and looked back. She was up on her paws and limping away when she heard his intake of breath and knew he'd spotted the endless black abyss.

Rain was up too, staggering and gasping. Dusk launched himself at her again, his roar more of a scream now, unleashing a series of wild slashes with his front paws that caught Rain's flank, and then turning on Leaf, a crazed fury glinting in his eyes. He crouched to spring, and then something else hit Leaf's side. It was Rain! She shoved Leaf out of the way, both of them rolling over and over across the stone, and Dusk's claws raked the rock with an awful crunching sound.

He twisted and advanced once more, and Leaf tried to stand, but her bitten leg twinged and she fell. She looked up at him, huge and terrible, silhouetted against the entrance to the cave once more, his eyes red and mad with fury.

Then something hit him from behind, and he stumbled and fell flat on his belly.

Ghost dug his claws into Dusk's back and bit down on his neck, like a snow leopard would do with its prey. He'd crept up behind Dusk with the grace of a predator, and now Dusk was screaming and writhing, trying to throw him off, and Leaf and Rain were scrambling to their paws and getting out of the way.

"Yeah, Ghost!" Rain called. "Get him!"

Leaf could see that Ghost was struggling. Blood streaked his white fur, and he wasn't going to hold on to Dusk much longer. But he was alive!

Dusk had to almost throw himself to the ground, but he finally hurled Ghost off his back. Ghost hit the stone floor with a thump, and Dusk tried to stamp down on his chest, but Ghost wasn't winded, and he rolled clear. Leaf leaped at Dusk's back before he could go after Ghost, scratching at him, and Rain was right beside her, going for the big panda's jaw with her claws. Dusk twisted to swipe at them, and his paw missed Leaf but hit Rain squarely in the face and launched her backward. She fell back, hit her head on the floor, rolled, and skidded on a smooth patch of rock, toward the edge of the chasm.

"No!" Leaf gasped, and ran to Rain's side, trying to grab her and pull her away from the abyss. Ghost was beside her too, his teeth in Rain's fur, and together they yanked her back from falling into the darkness. Rain blinked up at them, dazed but awake, and then her eyes focused over their shoulders and she let out a terrified whine.

Leaf spun around and found herself nose to nose with Dusk. She shuffled back a paw-length, but he had them all now, trapped between him and the endless fall into blackness. . . .

"You wanted to meet your precious Dragon?" he whispered. "How about I send all three of you to meet it right now?"

He raised a massive paw.

And then a flash of black and orange passed in front of Leaf's eyes, and Dusk was on the ground, and there, standing over him, muscular chest heaving, was an angry, snarling tiger.

"Shadowhunter!" she cried.

# CHAPTER TWENTY-ONE

"TIGER," DUSK SPAT, SCRAMBLING away as fast as he could. "Leave this place, or I'll finish the job Brawnshanks started!"

"Come on!" Ghost hissed to his sisters, and he half shoved Rain away from the edge of the chasm as the tiger—whose name was apparently Shadowhunter—stalked forward, his movements still graceful despite the blood that matted his fur.

*He's alive*, Ghost thought. *How?*

"I'm warning you," Dusk snarled again, as the triplets made it across the cavern floor to press themselves against the black rock wall. "You're half dead already; you're nothing. The pandas rule this kingdom, not the tigers!"

The tiger didn't reply for a few heartbeats. He circled Dusk, tail low to the ground, moving like a predator, his eyes bright and fixed on his prey.

"We are the Watchers. We are the eyes in the darkness," Shadowhunter said at last, still circling Dusk, his voice low and calm but seeming to fill the whole cavern. "We are the paws of the Dragon, and its teeth. We come when we are needed. I am here to fulfill my oath, to make sure that the triplets take their rightful place as the Dragon Speakers of the Bamboo Kingdom. I was Sunset's Watcher," he growled, a flash of emotion in his voice, "and I failed him. I will not fail again."

Dusk leaped, and Shadowhunter sprang to meet him. They clashed in midair, gnashing teeth at each other's throats, heavy paws striking hard, blood spattering against the black stone floor. They pulled apart and then pounced again. Dusk landed awkwardly, one leg crumpling under him, unable to bear his weight. . . .

"Come on, Shadowhunter," Leaf murmured beside Ghost. "What happened to him?"

"He saved me," Ghost said. "From the monkeys. I thought he'd died!"

*How, how is he still alive?* he thought.

Ghost was watching for any moment where he could leap in, where he could help, and he felt Rain beside him twitching as she thought of rushing forward, but stopped herself. The tiger and the big panda were too well-matched, moving too fast—if any one of the triplets ran into the fray, they'd be just as likely to be clawed by Shadowhunter as Dusk.

Shadowhunter lunged for Dusk's throat, but Dusk ducked his head just in time. The tiger's teeth ripped a long, bloody tear from his cheek. Dusk wrenched himself to one side, sending Shadowhunter sprawling on the rock, close enough to the mouth of the abyss that all three triplets gasped.

Then Dusk was on his paws again, balancing on three with his injured one dragging behind him. He gave another roaring scream of unbound rage, and pounced. Shadowhunter flicked his tail into Dusk's eyes, and that was just enough distraction for the tiger to wriggle out from underneath Dusk. The huge panda landed on the stone with both front paws, making a thud that resonated around the cavern. The pressure could have crushed the rib cage of an animal who'd been lying on that spot. Ghost thought he heard claws snap.

As Dusk struggled to turn, hobbling on bruised paws, Shadowhunter paced back a few paw steps.

He took in Dusk's position, and then looked over at the triplets, his gaze finding each of them in turn. He gave a deep bow.

For a moment all Ghost could see was Winter, falling into the Endless Maw, her tail lashing, paws splayed, in the moments before the awful, final impact.

Then the tiger crouched, pounded across the black stone, gathering speed, and sprang. Shadowhunter's paws struck Dusk's flank, his jaws closed on the panda's neck, and he carried him over the edge of the chasm.

Rain and Leaf both ran to the edge, shouting Shadowhunter's name. Ghost followed them, on stumbling paws, just in time to see the two figures, locked in battle, falling until they were swallowed entirely by the darkness. There was no thump of snow. No sound at all. They were just . . . gone.

"Shadowhunter," Leaf moaned, falling onto her belly on the edge of the chasm.

Rain took a breath, as if to speak, and then let it all out in a heavy sigh.

"He gave his life for ours," Ghost said.

"He was the best Watcher we could have asked for," Rain said at last. She peered over the edge and spoke directly into the darkness. "You didn't fail us, Shadowhunter. Your oath is fulfilled, a hundred times over."

Silence fell in the cavern. Ghost sat back on his haunches, exhausted. For a long moment, there was nothing but the soft breathing of his sisters and the aching pain that seemed to fill up his whole body.

Then Rain said, "Um," in a tone that made Ghost's heart skip a beat. "Is that . . ."

"Get back!" Leaf sprang to her feet and pushed Rain away from the edge of the abyss. They bumped into Ghost, and all three of them sprawled and scrambled back, as something began to rise out of the darkness of the chasm.

But it wasn't something . . . it *was* the darkness, like a cloud made up of pure shadow. It burst from the ground and began to swirl around the cavern, filling it in moments, like trailing fog, or smoke. It blocked out the light at the peak and covered the cave mouth, plunging the three triplets into total darkness . . . except that Ghost could still see his sisters, and more than that, he could *see* the coils of darkness moving around him, winding over and around each other.

*The Great Dragon. It's here, with us!*

It should have been terrifying to be in the coils of something so inconceivably vast. But it wasn't. He could see flashes of shapes gleaming in the darkness: glimpses of vast scales, like afterimages against his eyelids from looking at the sun too long. They were dazzling and fleeting, but *real*. His heart rattled in his chest, but all he felt was simple, total awe. The coils slowed and stopped. Ghost instinctively stepped close to Leaf and Rain, and felt their warm, solid shoulders pressed to his, too.

Then light flared all around them, and Ghost had to shut his eyes against the glare. Slowly, he pried them open.

The Great Dragon had shining scales of red and gold, almost too bright to look at, shimmering with their own internal light. It had golden talons like a bird's, deep red spines along its back, and golden hair curling from its tail.

The Dragon was here, and it was *glorious*.

Ghost looked up, and saw a vast face looking down at him— the jaws of a snake, the whiskers of a tiger, and bright, pupilless golden eyes that burned like suns. A mane of hair the color of the stars danced and flowed around its head, always moving.

Ghost had never felt so small.

The Dragon moved through air as if it were water, its coils shifting around the three small pandas, rainbow reflections flashing from its scales like the reflections from the underground lake.

Ghost heard Leaf's breath catch in her throat, and felt Rain's heaving shoulders relax, going soft and still against him.

He looked into the Dragon's burning eyes and saw . . .

A panda picking her way through swirling snow. She collapsed, shuddering, the tiny white bundle falling from her jaws. With an effort that he knew, deep in his heart, would soon cost the panda her life, she picked up the mewling cub and walked on.

Orchid was lost in the swirling brightness, but then he saw another face: Winter, bending her head to lick at a shivering white cub, curling herself around it to save it from the cold.

Then he saw Snowstorm and Frost and Shiver, just born, still blind, snuggling up close to him in Winter's den. There he was, walking over the mountains, growing bigger and stronger, but never understanding his place. There were the paw prints of the Snow Cat, leading him to his prey . . . and for a moment he *saw* what had left those prints, the long body winding across the mountainside.

*You are the same,* he thought. *You are the Snow Cat; you always were. . . .*

There were the sun bears, watching him leave with his littermates. There was Ghost sitting at the edge of the Endless Maw, dark thoughts swirling around him like the snow, and there was Winter falling, and there were the Prosperhill pandas, Dusk, Pepper, the monkeys. He saw them all, and then he saw the Bamboo Kingdom, as if he were flying over it. He saw the rolling hills and deep valleys, the peaks of the mountains, the river running through the middle like the shining body of the Dragon itself. For a moment he thought he could sense every creature moving in the kingdom, from the ants to the tigers. . . .

Then the Great Dragon blinked, and Ghost was back in the cave. He caught one last glimpse of it in all its glory. Its terrifying, wonderful face was filled with delight as it gazed down on the triplets.

And then it winked out, like a flame, and was gone.

Ghost gasped, as the cold and dark rushed back into the cavern, leaving him shuddering. By the time his eyes had readjusted to the darkness, the coils of shadow had vanished, maybe back into the chasm, maybe simply into the air.

Ghost turned to look at Rain and Leaf, and saw the same slack-jawed shock on their faces that he felt on his own. None of them spoke for a while. Ghost supposed there wasn't really anything to say. They had all seen it.

"Dragon ritual," Rain finally said, and Ghost felt himself relax, as if saying the obvious out loud had actually helped.

"What now?" Leaf said.

"And what do we do with *that*?" Rain added. Ghost turned to look where she was looking.

The white light of the snowy mountainside spilled into the cavern and caught something blue, glowing on the floor of the cave. It was the stone. Ghost stared at it—he had no idea when he had lost it, or how it had gotten here, but here it was.

The triplets approached it, and Ghost reached out a paw to touch it.

*Crack!*

The blue stone rocked and splintered, and fell apart. Ghost jumped, horrified, before he realized that it had split neatly into three equal sections, which rocked back and forth on the stone, one at the paws of each panda.

"Dragon Speakers." The voice rang out all around, and all three of them jumped. "You speak for the kingdom. You speak for me. You need not speak always with one voice—that is your strength, and my design."

Ghost felt a shiver run down his back as he thought of the voice coming from that vast, golden face. It was high and fluting, like wind through the trees, and deep and growling like rolling rocks, all at the same time. It seemed to echo in the cavern, but he couldn't help wondering if anyone but the triplets would have been able to hear it.

He looked back at his siblings, and then down at the three stones. They had changed color, as if splitting in three had released the colors he had seen dancing in the depths of the single stone.

"The blue stone is for you, Speaker Rain," the Dragon said, "who swims between worlds, Speaker for the the waters and the moon. The green stone is for you, Speaker Leaf, who climbs to the highest branch, Speaker for the trees and the sun. And the white stone is for you, Speaker Ghost, who walks with hunters, Speaker for the mountains and the stars."

Ghost reached out and pulled the glimmering white stone toward him. The way the light played over its surface looked like the swirling of a snowstorm.

"The Bamboo Kingdom needs each of you," the Dragon said, and now its voice gave Ghost chills for a whole different reason—a dark, serious tone filled the cavern. "Great danger rises, and more than the forest will be broken before it's done. The harmony of our world is fragile, and all three of you will be needed.

"Now go," it said, and its tone lightened a little. "Walk out into the world, my Dragon Speakers, and know that I will always be at your side."

# CHAPTER TWENTY-TWO

RAIN STEPPED OUT OF the cavern, blinking in the daylight, the blue stone held tight with her grip pad, where it seemed to fit so perfectly that she couldn't imagine ever wanting to put it down.

Everything felt so different. The sun was shining out over the Bamboo Kingdom down below, wispy clouds casting shadows as they moved over the hills. Fresh snow covered the path down the mountain, hiding the places where they had slipped, fallen, and bled. Rain's wounds ached, and she was sure that Ghost must feel much worse, but she knew it was going to be all right. The Dragon was with her. It had looked like a sunrise, and its voice had sounded like the crash of water rushing over rocks. She'd seen her life pass through its eyes.

*It's real—much more real than I thought it would be!*

She still wasn't really sure what being a Dragon Speaker would be like, but with the Dragon at her side, she knew she would work it out.

"What should we do now?" Ghost said.

"We go home," Leaf told him. She stared out over the kingdom, as if she were seeing it for the first time. "We listen for the Dragon's words, and protect the Bamboo Kingdom as best we can."

"All right," Rain said. "But first we find some bamboo as soon as possible. I'm starving."

"Oh *yes*," said Ghost. "Yes, please. I haven't had bamboo in days."

"How many feasts have we missed now?" Leaf asked.

"I don't even know," Rain said, leading the way down the winding path. "But far too many!"

"One is too many," Leaf grumbled. "When I get home, I'm never skipping a feast again, not unless the whole Bamboo Kingdom depends on it."

Rain walked with much more confidence on the snow than she had on the way up—now that she'd fought off Blossom and Dusk on this path, she felt she didn't need to worry about just walking.

For a moment, thinking about Blossom, she was startled to see two figures standing in the snow at the bottom of the path. But neither of them was a panda.

*"Dasher?"* Leaf barked from behind Rain's head. She

squeezed past, half running and half sliding down the last few bear-lengths of the path. She caught the little red panda up in an embrace that took them both down, rolling over and over in the snow.

"Leaf!" Dasher squeaked. "I'm so glad you're okay!"

Rain stood aside and let Ghost squeeze past her and run to Shiver, who stood beside Dasher, needling the snow with her paws as her brother rushed up to her.

"Thank the Snow Cat," she said, winding all the way around Ghost, her fluffy tail tickling his nose.

Dasher flopped down in the snow and stared at the sky. "It's been a long, long couple of days," he said.

"You're telling me," Leaf said. "Look." She showed him the green stone held in her grip pad.

"So now you're *real* Dragon Speakers?" Dasher said, looking up at Leaf with wonder in his eyes. "You can actually *speak* to it and everything?"

"We could always do that," Rain said, grooming her paw. "But now it speaks back!"

"Sometimes," Leaf added quickly. "I think."

"How did you two get here?" Rain asked.

"We followed Shadowhunter," Shiver said. "He knew exactly where he was going. I went looking for Dasher, like I said, and I found him near the Broken Forest, with his healing bamboo, tending to Shadowhunter."

"That's how he survived the monkey attack," Ghost said softly.

Leaf laid an affectionate lick on Dasher's cheek. "You saved him—and he saved us," she said. "He defeated Dusk."

"But he's not here," Dasher said.

There was a sad silence, broken only by the whistling of the wind through the rocks.

"He knocked Dusk over the edge of a ravine," Rain said.

She saw Shiver give Ghost a startled look, her ears folding down in distress.

"I know," Ghost said quietly.

"They're both dead," Leaf said. "But Shadowhunter saved all our lives. We'd be gone, and there'd be no Dragon Speakers, if it weren't for him."

"And he avenged Sunset's death," Rain added. She thought of the panda she'd seen in the vision at the pool—resigned to his fate, but defiant at the same time. He'd wanted Dusk to know that even in death, he wouldn't be beaten.

*It feels weird, after spending so long mistakenly cursing his name—but I think I would have really liked Sunset Deepwood.*

"Let's get out of this terrible place," Dasher said. "No offense, Shiver. Red pandas aren't built for snow that comes up to their noses!"

"You can ride on my back," Leaf laughed. "I bet your tiny legs are tired! Oof—careful of the shoulder, though," she said, as Dasher climbed up and lay on her back.

"You all look like you could do with a pawful of purple leaf," Dasher said. "Maybe two. Let's go back to the place we found that bamboo, Shiver, by the stream."

"You found bamboo?" Rain asked, her stomach rumbling. "All the way up here?"

"Not quite—it was sometime yesterday. . . ."

They began the long walk down from the mountain, the five of them padding through the snow and clambering over the rocks, exchanging stories about what had happened to them in the last few days and what they thought might happen next. Rain found herself bringing up the rear, and as they climbed up out of the canyon, she turned back to look at the Dragon Mountain. Its black rock glowed as the sun dipped toward Long Light, almost like the glowing scales of the dragon in the darkness.

Then she turned again and gazed down toward the Bamboo Kingdom. Shadows were gathering in the valleys, and blue mist wreathed the hillsides. But the forests still blazed with green and gold.

She thought about how much had been lost. She thought about Sunset and Dusk—brothers who had ended up destroying each other. About Shadowhunter, Plum, Orchid, and all the others whose lives had been thrown out of harmony. Rain thought about every creature who had died in the flood—all those bones that lay under the river, the new spine that ran through the kingdom.

Restoring harmony would not be simple. Brawnshanks was still out there, well on his way to whatever his goal was, thanks to Dusk. He wouldn't be happy to hear that he had failed to put an end to the Dragon Speakers.

*Well, good. Let him rage and plot in his Broken Forest. The Dragon Speakers will be ready for him.*

Ghost called her name, and she hurried to catch up with the others as they made their way down the mountainside, toward the forest, and home.

# EPILOGUE

Nᴉᴍʙʟᴇᴛᴀɪʟ ɢʀɪᴘᴘᴇᴅ ᴛʜᴇ ʙʀᴀɴᴄʜᴇꜱ and leaned over to look down into the clearing, curling her tail around the tree for balance.

There were a lot of creatures down there, milling around with swishing tails and twitching ears. They'd obviously been drawn from all around, word traveling fast that something was about to happen. There were pandas and red pandas, obviously, gathered in solemn anticipation. There were two pangolins, standing up on their back legs, their front claws held in front of their chests nervously. There was a solitary manul cat sitting slightly apart, grooming its long fur and pretending not to be too interested. There were boars, and goats, and a takin, and a family of mice that kept the boar carefully between them and the manul.

She could smell the excitement from up here. None of them had noticed the lone monkey high up in the waving branches over their heads. Even the flying squirrels were too focused on the panda climbing up onto the flat rock in the middle of the clearing to notice that she was there.

No other monkey had come. No other monkey in the forest had dared to defy Brawnshanks's orders. But Nimbletail *had* to be here; she felt it somewhere deep down.

Pebble sat down on the rock and closed his eyes.

Another panda, who Nimbletail didn't know so well, was busily brushing moss off the surface of the rock, tutting to himself.

"We should have kept the sacred places in better condition," he muttered. "This rock used to shine. . . ."

"Come on, Juniper," said another one, nudging him away from the stone. "Let Pebble concentrate."

The animals hushed, and Nimbletail redoubled her grip on the branch and waited, staring at the young panda.

Then Pebble's eyes snapped open. For a moment he looked terrified. Then he started to smile.

"I can hear her!" he gasped. "It's Rain!"

He stared up into the trees, listening intently, and Nimbletail shrank back behind a spray of golden leaves, watching through the gaps between them as the branch she was sitting on swayed and danced in the wind.

"The triplets have come into their powers," Pebble said. "The three Dragon Speakers send a greeting, a promise, and a warning. They greet you all—Speaker Rain Prosperhill, Speaker Leaf Hollowtree, and Speaker Ghost Born of Winter."

An intake of breath, and then a chorus of celebratory hooting, whistling, mewling, and honking rose from the assembled animals. Pebble held up a paw.

"They promise to serve the Bamboo Kingdom, to protect all the creatures who live in harmony with the Dragon," he said. "And the warning: There's a storm coming from upriver, so those who live in the banks and near streams should be careful. She says—she says it's not a metaphor; it's going to rain, a lot," he added with a stifled laugh. He slumped a little on the rock and looked around at the other pandas with wonder in his eyes. Chatter and jubilation filled the clearing.

"Hail the Dragon Speakers," piped up one of the pangolins.

"We are entering a new era," said one of the goats, emotion making her voice crack. "It will be a time of peace, with the pandas to guide us once more!"

Nimbletail shrank back, hiding herself within the shadows of the tree.

*I wish they were right,* she thought.

She had to get back. She'd lingered too long here already, but she wanted to see what her rebellion had done. Ghost was supposed to die in the Broken Forest. Rain and Leaf were supposed to give up without the blue stone. None of this had gone as Brawnshanks had planned.

*But it won't be enough.*

She slunk away, leaping to the next tree, catching herself with her grasping fingers and her tail. Branches whipped past, and she became one with the rhythm of the wind in the trees, knowing just when to time her jumps and when to wait. She ran down the trunks and sprinted across the open, rocky slope up to the lip of the valley of the Broken Forest. She didn't like being out in the open. She always felt like something was watching her.

The Broken Forest was as dark as ever. She could see the storm clouds Pebble had mentioned blooming on the far side of the valley as she swung down between the splintered and fallen stumps of the trees. They had plenty of handholds and places to swing from, and many of them were even sprouting new growth, fragile twigs and dark leaves pushing up, trying their best to create a proper canopy. And there were plenty of insects to eat, and even some fruit. But it didn't feel like home, not like the lush forests south of the river.

Chattering and laughter carried through the trees, and Nimbletail swung toward the sound, landing on one of the stumps at the edge of the gathering that filled the central dip of the valley.

Perched on stumps, hanging from branches, lounging on the forest floor, for as far as Nimbletail could see, were the other monkeys. Hundreds of them.

She felt she should be glad to see them, excited to talk to distant family and meet new friends. But with Brawnshanks in charge, here in the Broken Forest he'd been so obsessed with for so long, the sight of her fellow monkeys only made her shiver.

*This isn't a family,* she thought, looking down into the valley. *This is an army.*

Thunder rumbled overhead, and Nimbletail felt the first heavy drops of rain against her back.

The storm foretold by the Dragon Speakers was coming.

# ENTER THE WORLD OF
# WARRIORS

## Check out WarriorCats.com to

- Explore amazing fan art, stories, and videos
- Have your say with polls and Warriors reactions
- Ask questions at the Moonpool
- Explore the full family tree
- Read exclusives from Erin Hunter
- Shop for exclusive merchandise
- And more!

## Check Out the New Warrior Cats Hub App!

Download on the
**App Store**

GET IT ON
**Google Play**

**HARPER**
*An Imprint of HarperCollins Publishers*

warriorcats.com • shelfstuff.com

# ARE YOU A TRUE ERIN HUNTER FAN?
# READ THEM ALL!

## THE PROPHECIES BEGIN
- Into the Wild
- Fire and Ice
- Forest of Secrets
- Rising Storm
- A Dangerous Path
- The Darkest Hour

## THE NEW PROPHECY
- Midnight
- Moonrise
- Dawn
- Starlight
- Twilight
- Sunset

## POWER OF THREE
- The Sight
- Dark River
- Outcast
- Eclipse
- Long Shadows
- Sunrise

## OMEN OF THE STARS
- The Fourth Apprentice
- Fading Echoes
- Night Whispers
- Sign of the Moon
- The Forgotten Warrior
- The Last Hope

## DAWN OF THE CLANS
- The Sun Trail
- Thunder Rising
- The First Battle
- The Blazing Star
- A Forest Divided
- Path of Stars

## A VISION OF SHADOWS
- The Apprentice's Quest
- Thunder and Shadow
- Shattered Sky
- Darkest Night
- River of Fire
- The Raging Storm

**HARPER**
*An Imprint of HarperCollinsPublishers*

warriorcats.com

# ARE YOU A TRUE ERIN HUNTER FAN?
# READ THEM ALL!

## THE BROKEN CODE
- Lost Stars
- The Silent Thaw
- Veil of Shadows
- Darkness Within
- The Place of No Stars
- A Light in the Mist

## A STARLESS CLAN
- River
- Sky
- Shadow

## GRAPHIC NOVELS
- Graystripe's Adventure
- Ravenpaw's Path
- SkyClan and the Stranger
- A Shadow in RiverClan
- Winds of Change
- Exile from ShadowClan

## GUIDES
- Secrets of the Clans
- Cats of the Clans
- Code of the Clans
- Battles of the Clans
- Enter the Clans
- The Ultimate Guide

## NOVELLAS
- The Untold Stories
- Tales from the Clans
- Shadows of the Clans
- Legends of the Clans
- Path of a Warrior
- A Warrior's Spirit
- A Warrior's Choice

## SUPER EDITIONS
- Firestar's Quest
- Bluestar's Prophecy
- SkyClan's Destiny
- Crookedstar's Promise
- Yellowfang's Secret
- Tallstar's Revenge
- Bramblestar's Storm
- Moth Flight's Vision
- Hawkwing's Journey
- Tigerheart's Shadow
- Crowfeather's Trial
- Squirrelflight's Hope
- Graystripe's Vow
- Leopardstar's Honor
- Onestar's Confession

**HARPER**
An Imprint of HarperCollinsPublishers

warriorcats.com

# ARE YOU A TRUE ERIN HUNTER FAN?
## READ THEM ALL!

# SURVIVORS

**SURVIVORS**
- The Empty City
- A Hidden Enemy
- Darkness Falls
- The Broken Path
- The Endless Lake
- Storm of Dogs

**SURVIVORS: THE GATHERING DARKNESS**
- A Pack Divided
- Dead of Night
- Into the Shadows
- Red Moon Rising
- The Exile's Journey
- The Final Battle

# SEEKERS

**SEEKERS**
- The Quest Begins
- Great Bear Lake
- Smoke Mountain
- The Last Wilderness
- Fire in the Sky
- Spirits in the Stars

**SEEKERS: RETURN TO THE WILD**
- Island of Shadows
- The Melting Sea
- River of Lost Bears
- Forest of Wolves
- The Burning Horizon
- The Longest Day

**HARPER**
An Imprint of HarperCollinsPublishers

warriorcats.com

# ARE YOU A TRUE ERIN HUNTER FAN?
## READ THEM ALL!

**BRAVELANDS**
- Broken Pride
- Code of Honor
- Blood and Bone
- Shifting Shadows
- The Spirit-Eaters
- Oathkeeper

**BRAVELANDS: CURSE OF THE SANDTONGUE**
- Shadows on the Mountain
- The Venom Spreads
- Blood on the Plains

# BAMBOO KINGDOM

**BAMBOO KINGDOM**
- Creatures of the Flood
- River of Secrets
- Journey to the Dragon Mountain

**HARPER**
*An Imprint of HarperCollinsPublishers*

warriorcats.com